MW00909840

The Magical Adventures of Quizzle and Pinky Palm

Teresa Mae Waterland

Illustrated by Aletha Heyman

FriesenPress
One Printers Way
Altona, MB R0G 0B0
Canada

www.friesenpress.com

First Edition — 2023

Author photo: Gail Mead

"TT the Troll Too Tired to Trust" concept: Deb Palmer

ISBN
978-1-03-911537-8 (Hardcover)
978-1-03-911536-1 (Paperback)
978-1-03-911538-5 (eBook)

Juvenile Fiction
1. *Fairy Tales & Folklore*
2. *Action & Adventure*
3. *Fantasy & Magic*

Distributed to the trade by The Ingram Book Company

For my dear wife, Gail,
who loves me into being every day!

Wags Cave
Quizzle's Hive
Pinky's Burrow
Garden of Everywhere
Rock Quarry
TT's Bridge
Justaroundthebend
Tree Forest
Guardian Grove
Rollicking River
Garden of Everywhere
Redbush Ranch
Lay of the Land

Table of Contents

Auntie Hoolahoop Goes Missing

Chip, chip, crunch—chip, chip ting.... Quizzle, a feisty little fairy with spikey red hair and her dear friend Pinky Palm were at the rock quarry. They were helping Quizzle's Auntie Hoolahoop look for purple crystals—amethyst crystals, to be precise.

Chip, chip, crunch—chip, chip, ting.... Each type of crystal carried its own special essence, and Auntie used these in her magic spells, as most fairies did. These particular purple crystals carried just the right dose of humility. According to Auntie, one could never quite get enough of this ingredient.

In fact, humility was one of the qualities Quizzle most admired in Pinky Palm. Pinky was not a fairy. He was one of a kind, and not at all, really. You see, Pinky Palm was an *everyanimal*.

"What is an everyanimal?" one may ask. An everyanimal has the gift of seeing the world from many perspectives, not just their own. Everyanimals have a way of putting themselves into the hearts, paws, talons, and even the shoes of others, as if they were actually them. Suffice it to say, Pinky Palm cared deeply for everyone and everything. On most days, however, he looked most like a gopher wearing glasses—a teeny, tiny gopher—his *homebody*.

"What is a homebody?" one may ask. Well, a homebody is the body in which an everyanimal feels most at home. For Pinky, being a gopher fit the bill. He loved digging tunnels, his favourite foods were red berries and nuts, and he was an ever-curious sort.

Chip, chip, ting.... Amidst the dust and the muck, and the sparkle and glint of the crystal quarry, one could spot Auntie Hoolahoop with a tiny pick in her hand, looking here and there. She was a round cuddly sort, with rosy-pink cheeks and purple and green hair. Chip, chip, ting, ting.... The threads from her multicoloured skirts glistened in the sun as she ambled here and shuffled there, chipping out the most perfect amethyst crystals she could find. Auntie Hoolahoop was just bending over to retrieve such a gem when, all of the sudden, she let out a resounding, "Oh my dear!"

Quizzle and Pinky looked up quickly from their search. They could see that Auntie had gotten her wing caught, and her voice was frantic with alarm. But even so, Auntie Hoolahoop remained very still, and very upside down, afraid she'd lose the wing all together.

"Help!" she called to Pinky and Quizzle. "*He-ll-lp*!"

Quizzle flew over to her auntie, and Pinky Palm was right behind.

"Oh, look, Pinky!" Quizzle exclaimed. "Auntie Hoolahoop's wing is caught between two rocks!"

"A rock and a very hard place," quipped Auntie Hoolahoop as she regained just a little of her sense of humour. Pinky, Quizzle, and Auntie Hoolahoop were all very puzzled. In fact, they were in a tizzy. *What to do? What to do!*

Pinky forced himself to sit down quietly beside Auntie Hoolahoop. He needed to calm down and think this out. Pinky thought, and he thought hard. Then he thought some more.

Quizzle tried to calm her auntie with reassuring twittery words, such as, "It's going to be okay, Auntie!" and, "We'll get you out of here in no time, you and your wing."

Suddenly, Pinky had an idea. "Oh,

oh! Okay!" Pinky said. "How about if I push and you pull, until we move this big rock just enough to get your auntie's wing free?"

Auntie Hoolahoop gave a worried sigh and then whispered the familiar words: "Oh my! Oh my!"

Pinky wrapped his long, ginormous, fluffy tail around the big rock and pulled and pulled. Quizzle put her wings into high gear, and she pushed and pushed.

Perhaps Pinky had pulled too hard, or maybe Quizzle had pushed too hard, but the long and the short of it was that Auntie Hoolahoop went flying, but not on purpose. Like a rocket ship, she shot right up out of the quarry in a flurry of wings, wands, and whispers!

"Oh, my goodness gracious!" she exclaimed helplessly to the treetops as she shot right past them.

Pinky and Quizzle could only watch with dismay as Auntie Hoolahoop *splurched* through a damp cloud and disappeared from view. Quizzle looked at Pinky, and Pinky looked at Quizzle. Neither said a word. They were struck speechless. Quizzle gazed back at the rocks, trying to understand just what had happened. The larger rock cracked and moaned like old bones as he peeked around from behind himself to give Quizzle and Pinky a deeply apologetic look.

"I'm sorry," Rock said, and then he turned away again.

Quizzle noticed a twinkle and a glint from a small crevice in the large, sorry Rock.

"Oh no!" she cried. "Look, Pinky. It's Auntie Hoolahoop's left wing!"

And sure enough, there it was: Auntie Hoolahoop's left wing, still quivering in a crevice. Quizzle gently picked up the translucent purple and green wing and placed it securely in the folds of her cloak.

"We have to find her!" she whispered to Pinky.

Quizzle and Pinky were at a total loss as to how to find Auntie Hoolahoop. As they were thinking, Hummingbird and Dragonfly appeared, their wings all abuzz. Hummingbird's throat flashed red, and Dragonfly's blue eyes twinkled. Quizzle sighed with renewed hope as she spotted these beautiful creatures, all aglisten with shades of green and midnight blue.

Hummingbird and Dragonfly had some news to share.

"We were sipping—" Hummingbird said.

"—and dipping," Dragonfly said.

"Down at the marsh—" Hummingbird explained.

"—we heard a big flurry," Dragonfly declared.

"Then what happened?" Pinky asked.

"We looked up!" both declared in unison.

Hummingbird and Dragonfly had a way of finishing each other's sentences.

"What did you see?" Quizzle asked. She was growing a little impatient with the time it was taking for her two dear friends to spit this story out.

"Auntie—!" Hummingbird said.

"—Hoolahoop!" Dragonfly buzzed in.

Indeed, they had both looked up to see Auntie Hoolahoop awkwardly pitching, rolling, and yawing her way over the treetops with one wing and a kindly eagle's feather. Perhaps a kindly eagle lent it to her. She was so high in the sky though, that neither Hummingbird nor Dragonfly could reach her.

"She was too far up," they reported in unison, "she was higher than high!"

Using their keen sense of direction, however, they were able to estimate, based on her current trajectory, that she would likely make a forced landing somewhere near Redbush Ranch. The thought of a forced landing caused Hummingbird to fluff up in midair, and Dragonfly's eyes opened wide.

"Oh, thank you Hummingbird and Dragonfly!" cried Quizzle. She was relieved to hear that her auntie was still relatively okay.

Pinky Palm, Quizzle, Dragonfly, and Hummingbird put their heads together, and with a whirr and a buzz, a twinkle and a whistle or two, they decided to rescue Quizzle's auntie right away. Pinky Palm led the way as they climbed out of the quarry and onto the path that led through Tree Forest.

They followed Pinky as he leapt and bounded over rocks and bushes, and around the much larger spruce and pines. They followed Pinky as he scaled cliffs and tunnelled his way through bracken and slime. They followed him over hill and dale. Pinky had an excellent sense of direction and was an accomplished pathfinder for his young age, so the others were all too happy to let him lead.

Quizzle, Hummingbird, and Dragonfly couldn't help but admire Pinky's impeccable grace, nimble footing, and fearless free-falling as he led them along. Pinky could run, Pinky could jump, and Pinky could leap from high places. At times, Pinky had the most beautiful fur, each bristle capable of reflecting any colour of the rainbow, depending on his mood. Some moments he seemed more like a lion, and when he was feeling small in the grand scheme of things, more like a mouse. They each could see themselves in his reflection at different times. Hummingbird admired his hum, and Dragonfly respected the way Pinky could fearlessly set himself down—unnoticed—on the back of an alligator sleeping in a sunny marsh. Quizzle too adored her dear friend from every angle, but what she loved most about Pinky was his warm heart.

Pinky left a lot to the imagination and yet nothing at all, really. Pinky was simple, humble Pinky Palm. By now one may have guessed that his palms were pink. What one might not know is that they got that way from eating red berries.

With a whistle and a trill from Pinky, they all came to an immediate halt. Pinky had stopped; now he stood on his hind legs and sniffed the air while making quick little boxing motions with his two front paws.

"What is it, Pinky?" Quizzle whispered as she fluttered by his ear.

"I'm not sure," Pinky whistled, "but something smells familiar."

Quizzle, Dragonfly, and Hummingbird all took a big sniff... just as Skunk came out, her tail in the air!

"Oh, hello, Skunk," they chimed politely. The friends tried to smile and choke back their coughs as their faces turned green. The scent grew more putrid the closer Skunk got. They didn't want to hurt Skunk's feelings, but oh, if they could just get Skunk to keep her distance and not stand so close. Skunk, unfortunately, appeared to want to stop and talk. She looked like she might have some news. The foursome continued to brace themselves and to hold their noses as politely as they could, awaiting what Skunk had to say.

"Sorry, you guys. I didn't know you were coming," she said, waving her tail here and there. "If I had known, I would have cleared the air." She smiled sheepishly—or was it a sarcastically-motivated grin? It was always hard to know just where Skunk was heading, but it was very easy to tell where she had been.

"I went to Redbush Ranch for a little nap in the barn," Skunk said. "Just as I was waking up, I heard quite a commotion."

She had sidled out and up one side of the barn to see what was going on. She peeked around just in time to see Auntie Hoolahoop coming in for a landing. She watched in amazement as Auntie Hoolahoop *pitched and scritched* her way over the treetops. Then, she witnessed in horror as Auntie Hoolahoop bounced and slid her way over the hayfield, narrowly missing a scarecrow, which was waving wildly in the wind. She plowed straight through a haystack only to land with a plop, plop, and a drop.

"She landed right under Mrs. Grupple's nose!" Skunk exclaimed.

"Who's Mrs. Grupple?" Quizzle questioned.

"A sleeping yellow dog," Skunk replied matter-of-factly.

"Where's Auntie Hoolahoop now?" Pinky asked.

"Under...the...nose...of...a...sleeping...yellow...dog." Skunk spoke slowly and carefully, like a teacher wanting a student to get it right. Finally, they got it!

With this latest news, Quizzle became frazzled. Her wings flew in opposite directions as she spun herself into a real tizzy. Hummingbird stopped humming and dropped to the ground in shock. Dragonfly froze in midair, and Pinky whistled loudly. Pinky's whistle, which at first suggested disbelief, changed after a second into a call-to-attention kind of whistle. They all stopped and looked at Pinky.

"Well," Pinky stuttered, looking for the right words to say. "At least...

the yellow dog is sleeping!"

Pinky had a way of seeing the best in things. With this hopeful thought, Hummingbird rose up again, Dragonfly went back into motion, and Quizzle regained firm control of her wings.

"Which way to Redbush Ranch?" Pinky asked Skunk. "We need to get there before the sleeping yellow dog wakes up!"

"The way I came," she replied.

With that, they all knew they would have no trouble finding the route. Suddenly, Skunk didn't smell so bad to her desperate friends. Off she went one way while Pinky, Quizzle, Hummingbird, and Dragonfly went in the other direction.

"Thank you, Skunk!" Quizzle remembered to say. Skunk, still within earshot, turned and waved farewell.

Meanwhile at Redbush Ranch, Auntie Hoolahoop contemplated her predicament. There she was, her purple and green hair in a mess and her skirts all askew, lying under the nose of a sleeping, yellow Labrador Retriever with bad breath.

How on Earth did I get myself into this mess? she wondered without a word. *No, no,* she thought. *The real question is how do I get myself out from under the nose of this pooch without waking her up?*

Auntie Hoolahoop searched around for an answer outside herself but found none. She lay very still and yet very awake, painfully aware of every breath from the slumbering pooch. Mrs. Grupple breathed in, and then Mrs. Grupple blew out. Mrs. Grupple breathed in again... and then out. Every so often, her front paws would wiggle; she would *harruff* in her sleep and then breathe more quickly as if dreaming she was chasing a rabbit. Auntie Hoolahoop had 'let sleeping dogs lie' before, but never from quite this perspective.

It's curious, she thought, *how the world can look so different depending on where you're standing, flying, or lying, as the case may be.*

Back in the forest, Quizzle felt an urgent flutter under her robe. It was as if her Auntie Hoolahoop's left wing was telling her to hurry up. She touched the wing gently and whispered to herself, "We will save her. Everything will be okay soon."

Finally free of Skunk's scent, Pinky took a breath. He stood at the edge of a cliff and peered down at Redbush Ranch. All he could smell now was the sweet smell of a hay fart on a fall breeze. Likely, this had come from the resident horse.

"I see your auntie!" he cried. "Oh my! Skunk was right. She's under that dog's nose, all right!"

Pinky's eyes opened wide and Quizzle took a deep, worried breath. Hummingbird stopped humming, and Dragonfly's buzz came to a halt. They were all so afraid in that moment; they didn't know what would happen if Mrs. Grupple woke up!

"We have to get down there now!" Pinky cried. There was just one small problem: this was a very high cliff. Without wings, Pinky couldn't fly as the others could.

Pinky looked at his friends. "You go ahead," he said with brave determination, and Quizzle, Dragonfly, and Hummingbird knew they must. Off they went, their wings all abuzz. Pinky wasted no time either as he scrambled over rocks, around bushes, and down the cliffside to catch up.

Arriving at Redbush Ranch (and very close to her auntie now), Quizzle felt a squeeze in her heart. She set herself down, ever so lightly, on a stack of hay that was not far from Mrs. Grupple and the uncommonly quiet Auntie Hoolahoop.

Hummingbird and Dragonfly hung nervously in the air near Quizzle, waiting and wondering what to do next. Looking around, they could see a log cabin with a big porch. This was likely the dog's home, but the door was shut tight. On the porch was a dish with big letters painted on it. The letters spelled out MRS. GRUPPLE, but the dish appeared to be empty—not a good sign. Also on the porch were a stack of pumpkins, two barrels of what looked to be yellow beans, and a basket of snowballs.

It was fall, and Halloween was not far away. While it might seem strange to some, here it was not unusual to have snow in the mountains by fall. Nevertheless, Hummingbird and Dragonfly were a little curious about the snowballs. They wondered: Who had made them? Who was planning to use them? For what purpose? and Why? Quizzle, on the other hand, thought the snowballs were the least of their worries.

Auntie Hoolahoop turned her head ever so slightly, careful not to wake Mrs. Grupple. Her purple and green hair stood on end. When she spotted her dear niece Quizzle and her friends Dragonfly and Hummingbird hovering near the haystack, she breathed a sigh of relief and her hair relaxed. Auntie Hoolahoop resolved to wait patiently.

Once again, Quizzle and her intuitive friends put their heads together, but this time not a whistle or a whirr could be heard. Silence was of the utmost importance. It was not the *you-better-be-quiet* kind of silence. It was the kind of silence that hides a secret. They thought as one, and their thoughts were wordless and wise. It wasn't quite clear what plan they had come up with, but they did have a plan.

The problem was they didn't get to use it—Mrs. Grupple woke up!

Suddenly Mrs. Grupple opened both of her big brown eyes. She was puzzled by what she thought she saw. She closed her eyes again and shook her head. Then she slowly opened one eye. She was still confused. She opened her other eye. What she thought she was seeing was definitely bigger than a flea but smaller than a mouse.

Mrs. Grupple sniffed the air around Auntie Hoolahoop. Auntie Hoolahoop always smelled of lavender, and she was as colourful as any flower Mrs. Grupple had ever seen. Auntie Hoolahoop's purple and green hair and her multicoloured skirts shimmered in the crisp mountain sunlight. Completing her ensemble were a wing and a wand, which, given her inexperience with such matters, Mrs. Grupple confused for petal and stem. Mrs. Grupple loved petals and stems! She was always digging them up or knocking them from vases. She wagged her tail, which thumped the ground with growing excitement.

The thump of Mrs. Grupple's tail made Quizzle grow pale. Quizzle's blood chilled with the realization that she could lose her auntie altogether! She had to do something to distract this pooch—and it had to be soon!

Now, Quizzle was only a fledgling fairy. She hadn't even had her *flying up party*, and so she was not yet in full command of her wings. The terrible truth was that she wasn't quite sure what to do. She worried that even if she did *think* she knew what to do, it might not be the *right* thing. In fact, she was afraid she might get it all wrong and end up making things worse! Just as she was spinning herself into a sticky web of fear, she changed her mind. She decided to focus on her auntie instead.

With a heart full of love, Quizzle looked over at her auntie and simply forgot herself altogether. Whew, what a relief! Time seemed to stop for Quizzle and her friends. Then a magical light spread from Quizzle's heart, slowly bathing her entire little being in a luminescent display of pinks, blues, purples, and yellows, with just a hint of red. Her tiny arms reached out lovingly in Auntie Hoolahoop's direction as if to say, *I'm here, Auntie.*

From each of her twelve tiny fingers—six on each hand—stretched a ray of light as intense as the light from the brightest star. Despite her predicament, her beautiful little face was strangely calm. A peaceful smile graced her gentle mouth. Her spikey red hair held firm in the wind as the shimmering light danced all around her. Quizzle's little freckles were cuter than the spots on a ladybug's wing, and her teeny, tiny feet peeked out from her robe as she fluttered in the air. Quizzle, now a focused little fairy, had suddenly come into her power. She was a force to be reckoned with.

While all this was happening, Pinky Palm had crept onto the scene, trying to hide his huffing and puffing after his long run. Now Mrs. Grupple, Pinky Palm, Dragonfly, Hummingbird, and even Auntie Hooolahoop were spellbound by Quizzle. They forgot themselves completely as they focused on her brilliant light. Pinky, however, knew this wouldn't last for long. With one big, deep breath he leapt into action. Taking advantage of the moment, like he was heading for a home run, the brave Pinky Palm ran right under the dog's nose. He grabbed Auntie Hoolahoop by her skirts and hurled her high into the air away from Mrs. Grupple. Dragonfly and Hummingbird managed to catch her in midair before she crashed back to earth, and they flew her over to Quizzle, who smiled to them softly.

Quickly, Quizzle unfolded Auntie Hoolahoop's left wing from her flowing robes. Transforming just a little of her love into purple and green glue to match Auntie Hoolahoop's wing, she gently reattached it. Auntie rose even higher in the air with a great sigh of relief. It was the kind of sigh you sometimes hear from grown-ups after a long day on their feet when they finally get to sit down. Auntie Hoolahoop was airworthy once again!

Mrs. Grupple, too, had been riveted by this fantastic scene—until she caught a sideways glimpse of Pinky's bushy tail as he leapt up the porch step! He disappeared behind the stack of pumpkins, which rested next to the basket of snowballs and very near to one of the barrels of beans. Perhaps confusing Pinky for a teeny, tiny pooch who wanted to play, Mrs. Grupple immediately turned to give chase.

She bounded up the steps after Pinky, who now looked like he was in real trouble.

The others saw this and flew to his rescue, trying to distract Mrs. Grupple from her chase. Quizzle flew past Mrs. Grupple's nose. Hummingbird tried to block her view, and Dragonfly landed on Mrs. Grupple's back, busily buzzing loudly. Mrs. Grupple swung in circles, scratching wildly. With this commotion, even the fleas who called Mrs. Grupple home felt unnerved by these strange flying creatures; in a snit, they packed and moved out.

Despite the chaos of all these unfamiliar creatures—and her own fleas jumping ship—Mrs. Grupple kept her eye on Pinky and managed to continue her pursuit. She leapt to the top of the steps, her tail wagging wildly, and began nosing her way into the pumpkin pile. This time, however, Pinky was ready. First, he dug his warm little paws into the snowball basket. Then, he took aim. He sailed one snowball after another in Mrs. Grupple's general direction. Mrs. Grupple, who was used to playing ball, fetched for a while. She tried to bring the snowballs back to Pinky, but they melted in her mouth. Then she regained her doggy dignity and remembered her mission to catch that little dude!

Seeing the dog gaining on Pinky—Quizzle and Auntie Hoolahoop joined the fray. Auntie Hoolahoop went bowling with pumpkins, and Quizzle fired the beans. One might say they were all full of beans. Mrs. Grupple was just about to nab Pinky's protruding tail when a jack-o-lantern landed on the poor pooch's head! This was not quite what Auntie Hoolahoop had intended. Mrs. Grupple wildly swung her tail back and forth, in utter disbelief. Despite Quizzle's powerful radiance, one *swoosh* of Grupple's tail sent her flying. Pinky watched with alarm as Quizzle flailed by and smashed into a nearby tree.

"Ouch!" grumbled Quizzle to herself. "That hurt!"

"So sorry, miss," the tree whispered.

"Not to worry, I'll be okay," Quizzle said bravely, not wanting to cause the tree any concern. The determined Quizzle pulled herself right up onto the tree's strongest branch and began to survey the yard.

The sounds of grumbling, muffled barking, and crunching could be heard moving in her general direction. Quizzle peeked out from the protective leafy camouflage the tree had so generously provided, only to see Mrs. Grupple's tail wagging her way through the mess of snowballs, splattered pumpkin shells, and yellow beans.

"Oops," Quizzle whispered when she saw that Mrs. Grupple's head looked round and orange and her eyes were strange triangular shapes; this was not the pooch's usual features at all. It seemed that Mrs. Grupple had gotten herself into a real pumpkin! She chased her long bristly tail around in circles, and her usually loud bark echoed in her own ears now—more than in anyone else's—inside the pumpkin on her head.

Pinky Palm took this unexpected opportunity to make his escape. Although Pinky was most at home being a gopher, in this particular moment he didn't feel at home at all. In fact, he looked like a gopher in a big mess! Pinky needed a fast escape! Being ever so careful to avoid the spinning Mrs. Grupple, Pinky wound his way through the smashed-up snowballs and discombobulated pumpkins. He could almost taste the freedom he approached so cautiously.

Quizzle let out a soft *whistle* and *whirr* when she saw Pinky carefully avoiding the spinning Mrs. Grupple. Pinky looked up and felt relief as he spotted his friend on her perch.

Oh, good, he thought. *She made it!*

Pinky quickly waved at Quizzle, stepped over a large yellow bean, and scuttled across the yard towards the tree in which Quizzle had landed. Halfway across the grass, though, he turned back for just a moment to check on Mrs. Grupple. In one final, wild turn, Mrs. Grupple *smucked* her pumpkin head on the porch step with a tremendous thump. The jack-o-lantern cracked into pieces, freeing the astonished, breathless, and at least temporarily *barkless* pooch.

Mrs. Grupple let out a whimper, tucked her tail between her legs, and squiggled her way up the porch steps. She lay down and waited at the door of her mistress' cabin with her head hidden between her paws. And she ignored Pinky completely as he scooted along in double-time.

There was no need to worry much about Mrs. Grupple, though, as everyone in Tree Forest would find out later. Mrs. Grupple's momentary humiliation would give way to boastful memories of the time she fended off a hundred flying pumpkins and a swarm of what she thought were fireflies from Rough Patch Hollow. According to her story, she'd even managed to save Redbush Ranch from vicious snowballs and a whole barrel of marauding yellow beans! Yes, Mrs. Grupple had had a rough day indeed—a day she thought worthy of a big steak and a warm fire.

Pinky Palm arrived at the base of Quizzle's tree. He was all puffed out from his narrow escape and his run across the yard. Stopping to catch his breath, he thought about what to do next. He looked way up at Quizzle, who looked way down at him.

"Hi Pinky," Quizzle whispered and waved. Pinky smiled and waved back.

Quizzle felt a flutter and a tug on her back, which surprised her until she remembered her wings. She had been in such a flurry trying to interrupt Mrs. Grupple's chase that she hadn't even recalled using them. Quizzle's wings were thin and translucent like Dragonfly's wings, but fast like Hummingbird's. In fact, Dragonfly and Hummingbird were both invited to Quizzle's *flying up party* next summer.

Quizzle's confidence returned with the fluttering of her wings. She lightly rose from her branch, and with a sparkle and a twist barely visible to the human eye, she found herself hovering gently near Pinky Palm. The breeze from Quizzle's wings tickled Pinky's left ear and warmed his heart.

Auntie Hoolahoop waved over at the two. "Thank you, my dears!" she called out.

Dragonfly and Hummingbird dusted her off, then flew away waving goodbye. Quizzle and Pinky waved to their friends, then watched as Auntie lifted off on her own two wings. She flew a little off balance at first, and this surprised her until she remembered her pockets were full of purple crystals. She was more than delighted! They could hear her chuckle as she bid them adieu and disappeared from view.

“Let’s go home, Pinky,” Quizzle said. With a sigh of relief, Pinky nodded in agreement. Quizzle flew next to Pinky, keeping pace with his leaps and bounds as they headed across the hayfield towards Tree Forest.

Unlike many other forests, Tree Forest had been named after the trees themselves. The trees appreciated the recognition and prided themselves on providing shelter for a wide variety of magical creatures and critters. Anyone can leave Tree Forest, but without the secret password bestowed by the trees, one might, depending on one’s intentions, have a very difficult time getting in. Thankfully, Pinky, Quizzle, and the trees were old friends. Quizzle and Pinky whispered the secret word together: *raindrop*. The guardian trees bowed gracefully, welcoming the duo. Then a magical breeze offered them a ride. They hopped on and were warmly wafted through the friendly foliage and fauna. Seeing Pinky and Quizzle caused the foliage to bloom and the fauna to blink and wave at them in delight.

The friendly breeze carried them safely through the woods and over the marsh to the little-known village of Justaroundthebend. One had to squint one’s eyes just right to find one’s way into this quaint little hamlet. Resting on the warm, gentle breeze, Pinky and Quizzle enjoyed the view of their sweet hometown. From where they floated, they could see the gnomes in their log homes, fairies weaving magic in their hives, birds tending to their nests, and a wide variety of rodents peeking out of their burrows. Many of them waved up at Pinky and Quizzle as they sailed by. Then the magical breeze deposited Pinky on his welcome mat at the entrance to his family’s burrow. Pinky’s mother and father leapt up and bounded from their lookout post with a sigh of relief.

“Pinky, where were you?” they sputtered. Pinky just smiled at his parents, happy to be home.

“I’ll tell you all about it,” he whistled happily, “but first, could we go inside and have a snack? I’m famished!” Then, he gave Quizzle a little *I’ll-see-ya-later* nod, and Quizzle gave him a wave back with the tiniest flutter of a wing, smiling contentedly.

Soon, Quizzle's parents magically appeared, one on each side of her; unlike Pinky's parents, they didn't seem to have missed her at all. Was it possible they were with her the whole time? Well, not quite, but fairies do have secret ways of keeping tabs on their young.

Quizzle's parents were thrilled to have Auntie Hoolahoop home in one piece. In fact, they had prepared a welcome home feast! At the end of this adventurous day, it was time to make hay, so they all flew away.

Many of Quizzle's friends had never been to a flying up party.

Quizzle's Flying Up Party

Quizzle's family members were gathered in their fairy hive, which is like a beehive only much larger. They had all the comforts of home. Today, Quizzle's mother, father, and her Auntie Hoolahoop were busy preparing gift bags for Quizzle's *flying up party*. A flying up party was a bit like a birthday party, except it only happened once. The whole family had been taking great care to make sure everything was *just so*: Auntie Hoolahoop dropped three *party wishes* into each gift bag; Quizzle's father added magic fairy dust, being very careful not to spill a speck; Quizzle's mother added the *bless-you-dears* just in case any of the guests had to sneeze.

Quizzle had a long list of guests from all walks of life. This is not to say they were all walkers, of course, as some of them had feet that rarely touched the ground. Many of Quizzle's friends had never been to a flying up party. On the guest list were Pinky Palm, of course, and Hummingbird, Dragonfly, Millie Mole, Ricky Rabbit, Rock, and Skunk, who was a bit of a risk. Auntie Hoolahoop was invited as well, but she wasn't really a guest because she was family. All the trees of Guardian Grove were invited, too, but unfortunately, they had to decline by RSVP, explaining to Quizzle that they couldn't abandon their roots. Quizzle understood.

Also on the guest list was the whole town of Justaroundthebend, including Mayor Justintime and her family, Judge Justapeek, and all the other townsfolk.

Quizzle, who was alone in the woods, stood on a long, high branch of a tall pine tree. She was walking back and forth and back and forth, preparing for the big celebration. She wore her favourite play clothes. Most folks might be surprised to learn fairies are not always dressed in pretty frocks, but it is true. She had on a Mygosh pair of jean overalls. Around her wrist, she wore a multicoloured friendship bracelet woven for her by her dear friend Hummingbird. Pinned to her t-shirt collar was a little gold pin engraved with the inscription: *I love Pinky Palm*. For those who may be wondering, Quizzle's rainbow-coloured t-shirt had both armholes and wing holes. Her beautiful, translucent wings quivered with excitement, sending a chilly tickle down her spine.

Although Quizzle had sprouted her wings nearly a year ago, she still had some trouble controlling them, especially when she was nervous. She wanted to practice flying higher and higher without anyone seeing her until she got it just right. After a fairy's flying up party, they were expected to be in complete control of their wings, and there was no limit to how high they could go. Up until now, Quizzle hadn't flown very far at all, relatively speaking.

With her tongue sticking out to one side of her determined little scrunched-up fairy face, she very cautiously stepped further and further out towards the end of the tall pine tree's highest branch. Anyone who has ever learned to dive from the high board might have a slight inkling of what Quizzle was going through. However, there was no pool of water down below, which is not where she was going anyway. Quizzle planned to go up, definitely not down. Quizzle was glad to face this task alone. At least there was no one waiting at the base of the tree for a turn like they do at a diving board. She knew her wings were itching to fly, but she wasn't quite ready yet. Quizzle continued pacing back and forth and back and forth on her branch.

Back in his burrow, Pinky carefully wrapped up Quizzle's gift box. He had spent months working on this special surprise for Quizzle's flying up party. Pinky had decided to present Quizzle with a special gift to watch over her on her many flights without him, as he couldn't be with her all the time. Pinky couldn't fly, so he wanted Quizzle to have someone to watch over her while she was airborne. Quizzle didn't actually *need* anyone to watch over her, but Pinky didn't know this, and Quizzle truly enjoyed Pinky's protective nature. He sent in his order to The Gift Foundation months in advance and provided character references and proof of good intentions. Finally, he took a course on the care, feeding, and training of this particular gift.

The whole ordeal had taken up much of Pinky's summer vacation. The precious little gift just arrived yesterday on the Hound-Dog Bus where she had been cooped up for many long hours, so naturally, she didn't want to be cooped up again even though she was the gift. His gift kept jumping out of her box and running down one tunnel and up the next. There were just so many tunnels leading to Pinky's burrow!

Pinky was beginning to worry that his efforts had all been in vain. *What if the so-called little thing refused to behave at the party? What if she wasn't as advertised at all? What if she was an imposter?* Pinky worried so! Pinky had to calm himself down.

Pinky thought and thought. Finally, he was able to come to an understanding with the dear little gift. She could run around all the tunnels as much as she wanted, play with Pinky's stamp collection, and eat up Pinky's bag of nuts. She could lie in Pinky's hammock, which swung under his favourite tree. She could even read his favourite book! But only if she promised to jump into her gift box just before it was time to go to Quizzle's flying up party, and that was in two hours. The bejewelled little gift had no problem agreeing to all of these conditions.

Gently holding a wisp of her lovely lavender hair in crossed fingers, she swore a solemn promise to obey.

Meanwhile, Quizzle was still walking back and forth and back and forth on her branch. The pressure was mounting, and there were only two more hours to get it right. She had flown before, but never to such a great height. She knew the whole town and all her closest friends were coming out to share this special time with her, but right now she felt more nervous than special. What if she got her wings crossed? What if they started to fly in separate directions? What if she flew too close to a cactus, or even worse, too close to the sun? What if she forgot how to fly in midair? What if? What if? Quizzle's wings sometimes had a mind of their own, and they were growing impatient.

At about the same time, Skunk was in the barn at Redbush Ranch, resting up for Quizzle's flying up party. She desperately wanted to make a good impression, so she did something most skunks never do: she took a bath! In rose petals, no less. She had received her invitation to Quizzle's party two days ago, and she was secretly very pleased. She hadn't expected the invitation, as she rarely was invited to anything. Skunk remembered her friends holding their noses when she turned up in the woods. Skunk always acted like she didn't care, but the truth is she wanted to fit in. Although Skunk wasn't one to go on about things, she decided to have a chat with her own tail.

"Now," she said to her tail, fiercely wagging her finger, "I want you to *behave* at Quizzle's flying up party."

Skunk's big bushy tail stood straight up and came tip-to-tip with

Skunk's wagging finger, as if to say, *Want to see who's boss?* Skunk slowly lowered her finger, but her tail took the opportunity to strut its stuff, so to speak, and pretended to be sniffing all around in the air. Skunk's tail had to pretend because tails couldn't really sniff the air, and this was probably a good thing.

What Skunk and her tail didn't know was that just outside the barn door, Mrs. Grupple had heard her. Mrs. Grupple had excellent hearing, and this wasn't always a good thing. Mrs. Grupple had heard the news of Quizzle's flying up shindig, and when she realised that she wasn't invited, she felt her loyal canine heart drop out of its cage. Mrs. Grupple was wounded to the bone. She had *so* come to love those fireflies and their little gopher friend—or so she thought of them at first. Mrs. Grupple had never met a fairy before, and the closest thing she knew to fairies were fireflies. It was understandable that she had confused the two.

She loved them, even though they had stuck a pumpkin on her head. Of course, after the big debacle last fall, Quizzle and Pinky had checked in on the pooch. They had come to enjoy playing with Mrs. Grupple and she with them. Mrs. Grupple now completely understood how to behave around fairies.... Or did she?

The thing about Mrs. Grupple was that she had a big heart, and she never meant to harm. She had, however, so far in her short life, been given the impression that everything that moved was a toy. You might say that for Mrs. Grupple, it was always Christmas morning—but not today. Mrs. Grupple's tail sought small comfort tucked in between her hind legs. From behind the barn door, she watched with longing eyes as Skunk headed off toward the party, her two-toned tail in tow.

Quizzle's family had outdone themselves! Their hive was alive with sweet smells and magical music. The whole garden had been decorated with sprinkles, sparkles, streamers, and such. They had hired a little band, with big sounds, made up of tiny tooth fairies, with big grins, who worked all night and played all day. The long garden table was laden with every imaginable treat one could ever want; and if anyone couldn't find what they were looking for, all they had to do was make a wish and it appeared. The wishing well was full to the brim, and the delicate fairy-lace tablecloth waved gently in response to a newly arrived breeze. Floating and dancing in the sweet air were hundreds and thousands of bubbles, some of which were beginning to congregate in small groups. The scene was simply dizzying, and the guests were beginning to arrive.

First to arrive at the garden gate were Hummingbird and Dragonfly. They had agreed to arrive early to help welcome the guests. Hummingbird took their hats and Dragonfly buzzed off with their coats. Hummingbird was pleased to notice some of the guest's hats were laced with flowers.

Millie Mole nipped nervously at the little jingle bell that hung from the gate latch. She couldn't quite reach it. Auntie Hoolahoop flew over, lifted the latch, opened the gate, and swooped her up with welcoming arms.

"Hello, Millie, my dear," Auntie Hoolahoop chimed. "Quizzle will be so happy you came."

Millie handed her tiny gift to Auntie Hoolahoop. "It's quite small," she said with a twinkle, "but then so am I!"

"So are we all," said the wise, gregarious aunt. "So are we all, dear."

Then Ricky Rabbit hopped into the scene, and not a bit late. Along came Rock, who had rolled himself all the way from the quarry. He had managed to do this without gathering any moss. He did have a twig or two caught in one of his crevices, but these were easily brushed away by Quizzle's fairy mother as she offered him a place in the shade and a refreshing glass of dew.

Next came a loud drumroll from the Tooth Fairy Band, startling many of the guests, and in paraded the entire population of Justaroundthebend. Mayor Justintime led the procession, followed by her delightful flock of goslings and the town's gingerbread council. Mayor Justintime, a beautiful snow goose, always arrived *just in time*, as one might have guessed. Not far behind the goose, and fashionably late, came Judge Justapeek. Judge Justapeek was a strange, dodgy sort of character, but with an impeccable reputation. He was an Irish leprechaun with a nose redder than Santa's.

Soon Pinky slipped quietly through the gate, out of breath and looking a little worse for wear. He was carrying a jumpy little box to which he kept talking. Some of the guests thought this a bit strange.

And finally, last, but not least, came Skunk. At first, the guests looked slightly alarmed, but they relaxed as she wafted through the gate *smelling like a rose*. The party was about to begin!

Over on the other side of the forest, Mrs. Grupple was determined to join her newfound friends. She was now certain that her invitation had been lost in the mail. Without any luck, she tried to nose her way into Guardian Grove, the official entrance to Tree Forest. She tried to slip past a fern and wound up in some nettles. She tried to creep past a pine, but when a pile of cones landed on her head, she had to dig her way out.

One little wildflower piped up and said, "Use the password! Use the password!" But Mrs. Grupple didn't even know what a password was. She was stumped.

"What does a password smell like?" she wondered out loud as she sniffed around. *Perhaps someone dropped it*, she thought, her nose to the ground.

Quizzle had returned home and finished getting ready for her grand entrance. She had changed out of her Mygoshes and slipped into her tiny fairy frock, careful to let her wings out gently through the two dainty openings in the back. Done up in curls, her red hair was adorned with tiny sparkling jewels. She had on little dance slippers woven with gossamer thread. With barely concealed anticipation, Quizzle's parents waited to escort their beloved daughter out of the fairy hive they called home, and into her circle of friends.

The Tooth Fairy Band changed their tune to the traditional flying-up music. Enchanting tones filled the air, an intricate weave of both sound and silence. Fairies know just how much a single note is enhanced by the quiet within. Magical notes entwined with each other. They gradually increased in intensity and volume, then unfolded into a symphony of chimes reverberating throughout the land. They sent tingling sensations through the bodies of all the guests. Needless to say, the music was spellbinding. It was nearing time for Quizzle's ascent.

Quizzle was perched high on a branch above her adoring crowd, but what she was thinking, she could not say out loud! Her *what-ifs* were rising... *What if* she fell?! What if? What if?

Just as fear was about to win, she saw Pinky peeking from behind a tree with love in his eyes. Seeing her dear friend, Quizzle's confidence grew. Her wings tugged at her back. They had sensed a gentle breeze nearby and Quizzle could feel it, too. She turned and nodded to her wings, and with that, they unfolded to their full span. Sunlight shone through the translucent wings, and in them danced all the colours of the rainbow.

The breeze whispered in Quizzle's ear, "We can do this together. The time is now."

"Okay, let's go!" she said to the breeze and surrendered herself to the welcoming sky. Quizzle and her wings were now as one. She had all the confidence in the world, almost enough to forget herself completely. Up she went!

Ta! Da! Quizzle, all aglow, floated to the center of her ever-widening circle of friends. Suddenly, she knew this circle stretched all around the world, and indeed embraced many worlds. Her parents had not only given her the whole world: they had given her a universe.

Quizzle smiled with the gentle grace of a snowflake whirling across the sky, and she twinkled with the kind of sparkle one can sometimes see in kindly old eyes. Only Quizzle wasn't old—not in fairy years, anyway.

Quizzle smiled at Hummingbird and Dragonfly, dusting them with her magic. She waved at Skunk and nodded to Millie. She noticed every brave little soul who had ventured in his or her different way to this single place: The Garden of Everywhere. Then she looked for Pinky, who looked up shyly, hiding his tiny present behind his back. To Quizzle, Pinky himself was a present. He was to her the most special gift of all. He was the gift of friendship. She flew over to Pinky and placed a single *sacred wish* in his warm little paw. This wish was wrapped in a shiny blue gem. Pinky thanked Quizzle and tucked the sacred wish safely away. With this sacred wish, who knew what he would do?

Quizzle flew up higher. She rose above the treetops, and as the trees nodded their congratulations, a magnificent view of the whole forest opened to her. At the entrance to Tree Forest, however, sat one dear dog with a broken heart.

Oops, Quizzle thought, *I should have sent Mrs. Grupple an invitation.* Quizzle flew over to Mrs. Grupple. She looked deep into the pooch's eyes and whispered in her ear, "You are invited too, my furry friend!" As she whispered the secret password *raindrop* to the trees, Mrs. Grupple leapt with pure joy! Guardian Grove opened up, and she bounded down the path through Tree Forest toward the Garden of Everywhere.

From way above in the sky, she could hear Quizzle calling after her, "Remember you're a good girl, Mrs. Grupple, and be careful with Millie Mole." Mrs. Grupple proudly wagged her tail in acknowledgement.

Quizzle continued to rise above the clouds, rising even above the highest eagle. She couldn't help but notice in her flight that the kindly eagle was missing a tail feather.

"Say hello to your auntie for me," the eagle sang sweetly.

"Oh, indeed I will," Quizzle promised as she continued her climb. She soared above all the beings with branches, fur, talons, and paws until there was no one, no one at all. Here, Quizzle found she was very much alone. She had not yet become accustomed to the lack of oxygen, and for a brief second, she felt a little light-headed and feared she might faint. Because there was no one else with whom to speak, she resolved to chat with herself, thinking this might help keep her alert. She chatted herself right up through the ozone layer.

Soon she was floating in a shiny void of wordless darkness. Here there were only possibilities, and they were limitless and unimaginable. Quizzle gazed down at the Earth—or was it up? What she saw was a single organism, dancing in unison with itself. The Earth was as one body, populated with perfect little beings from the smallest ant to the tallest tree. The problem was, not everyone knew how perfect they were. All, or at least most, of these magnificent creatures had forgotten their *true natures*. Indeed, like waves in an ocean, they were each a different expression of the same thing—love.

"Oh my goodness!" Quizzle whispered to herself in awe. "Oh my goodness."

Back in The Garden of Everywhere, the guests danced, pranced, and chitchatted with each other. Many of them had never met one another before, as they lived in different places and in different ways.

Millie Mole had begun to relax, feeling the calming effects of the dew she sipped so delicately. She even found the courage to visit with strangers, the likes of whom she had never seen before. Millie Mole had come out of her hole, so to speak. She was particularly enjoying her time with Ricky Rabbit, whom she thought had the most handsome floppy-down ears and the cutest quivering little nose. Millie blushed when Ricky reached out his paw in courtly gesture, and with a flourish, asked her to dance the Hip Hop.

Quizzle's handsome fairy father gazed down the path that led into the woods, checking to make sure all was right. What he saw looked strange at first. He could see a yellow tail wagging its way through some tall grass. It was hard to know exactly what the tail might be attached to, but he could guess. He continued to observe as the tail grew nearer. And then, finally, he watched as Mrs. Grupple nosed her way out from between the blades of grass and into plain view. A hush fell over the crowd as she walked with extraordinary care up the path toward the garden gate.

Mrs. Grupple was so excited to be coming to the party that she could hardly contain herself, but she did. Tucked into her coat, she carried her favourite bone, a gift she was sure Quizzle would love as much as she did. Although the bone had been nibbled a bit here and chewed a bit there, it was a very special gift indeed. In fact, this bone was a wishbone, and Grupple hadn't used up the wish.

As Mrs. Grupple arrived, Quizzle's father was there to greet her. The little fairy, although dignified and sure of himself, was quite small in stature. Fluttering in the air by Grupple's nose, he bowed a generous welcome to Quizzle's newest-found friend, and then he opened the garden gate. Mrs. Grupple sniffed Quizzle's father ever so gingerly and gave her tail a polite little wag. Millie Mole, who had noticed Mrs. Grupple's arrival with some alarm, swooned into the arms of Ricky Rabbit, who carried her over to a shady spot where she could fan herself and catch her delicate breath.

Mrs. Grupple made her way into the party, ever so gently, greeting the guests one by one and being very careful not to jump on any of them. She soft-pawed her way over to Mayor Justintime, sniffed the beautiful goose in the appropriate place, and wagged her tail reverently. As she made her way past the mayor's entourage her tummy grumbled, but she was careful not to drool on any of the Gingerbread Council. Quizzle would have been so impressed had she seen this incredible act of good behaviour on the part of Grupple!

Well, Quizzle did see Mrs. Grupple! From where she floated, she could see everything. All dreamy and dappled with starlight, she smiled softly to herself. She was so blissful with blessings that her heart had to expand a little just to make room for all her love. Quizzle watched from above as her father guided Mrs. Grupple over to the treat-laden table. Grupple was so grateful! She had never before been offered a seat at a table! Mrs. Grupple's tummy gurgled happily as she began the best meal of her whole life.

Pinky Palm had watched the scene with warm-hearted surprise, but he was soon distracted by his jumpy little box.

"Let me out," coughed the bejewelled little gift from within. "*Let me out!*"

Pinky took pity on the poor cooped-up creature. He gently untied his gift. As Pinky lifted the golden lid, Quizzle magically appeared as if from nowhere.

"Oh, thank you, Pinky!" she exclaimed with a soft voice as she looked inside. Sitting in one corner of her little box, looking up at Quizzle, was the quirkiest little *guardian angel*! She was definitely one of a kind. One may recall Pinky had specially ordered her early in the summer. What one may not know is that she came directly from the Guardian Angel Foundation, a very reputable institution.

She had lovely lavender hair done up in a swirl, and her hazel eyes blinked rapidly in the sudden light. Although the little angel was trying to behave herself, she couldn't help but vibrate with excitement when she saw the kindly gaze of the young fairy peeking in at her. She looked up in amazement as Quizzle reached tenderly into the box to cradle her in hand. The guests, who had been watching this fantastic scene, whispered in awe at the remarkable gift Pinky had presented to Quizzle. They watched as Quizzle slowly lifted her Guardian Angel out of the box, and they gasped in unison as the hitherto cloistered little angel took the opportunity to *spring free*!

Now what they didn't know was that this guardian angel couldn't stand being cooped up. Like most angels, she needed a lot of space. At this point the opportunistic little angel's spring to freedom landed her squarely on the boot of Judge Justapeek, who had been conversing with others nearby. The judge, mildly irritated at the interruption in his conversation, shook her off. With just one shake of the judge's boot, the little guardian angel went flying; this was something she knew how to do very well.

Needless to say, Pinky was mortified. He was so embarrassed! He watched as his gift flew past some boisterous beavers bobbing for jellybeans. She flew furiously past noses and around feet. She flew here and she flew there. She flew right through Auntie Hoolahoop's hair. She took a swing on Mrs. Grupple's tail, but Mrs. Grupple just kept on eating. She hardly noticed as the little angel darted here and hovered there. Honestly, the way the angel was behaving, anyone might think it was *her* flying up party!

Quizzle, Pinky, and their friends were in hot pursuit. They reached and grabbed for the angel, hands and paws grasping the air. The whole gathering was astir, with feathers and fur flying here and flying there. The guardian angel would suddenly disappear behind a tree, only to pop up again under a knee. She flew circles around the guests, never stopping to rest. She flew over to the table of treats, scooping up a whole icing-covered cake, and when she was done, said it was all in fun.

"Weeee!" she screamed as she slid down a bean. "This is the best party I've ever seen! I've been cooped up for such a long time, and now I feel simply sublime."

Quizzle and Pinky, along with many of the other guests, were all puffed out from their chase. They couldn't help but laugh, however, as they looked at the angel's icing-covered face.

The Tooth Fairy Band played a new tune, and everyone joined in for the circle dance. They danced, slowly at first, then picked up their pace until the whole gathering magically spun itself into a blur of colour and sound.

Suddenly there was no one around! The party was over and a resounding success. A few kind friends stayed back to clean up the mess.

The whole gathering magically spun itself into a blur of colour and sound.

Pinky's Power

Pinky gazed with soft eyes into the clear mountain water that had settled itself into a quiet pool, near a stream that swept by. The water in the pool was still, not even a ripple. Pinky could see his own dear reflection as it shifted and changed. He saw his gopher *homebody* peering over the edge, with his brown, horn-rimmed glasses sliding down his nose.

He pushed the glasses back up and peered in once more. Though he could see his reflection, with which he was pleased, it wasn't his *Me* that he was longing to see. Pinky was just being his curious self. He was in a *wondering about this, pondering over that* sort of mood.

He wondered about Quizzle, and this should come as no surprise. The moment he thought of Quizzle, the pond reflected her eyes. *Wow!* thought Pinky. He gazed a bit longer, and soon he could see her flaming red hair. "Is that you, Quizzle?" he whispered. But no answer came from his feisty little fairy. *Hmm*, he wondered, slightly bemused and confused. *Wishful thinking, I guess*, he thought with a chuckle. Pinky was more than a little smitten with Quizzle.

Pinky continued to gaze into the water. It wasn't long before he could see a fish swimming around; not a big surprise. The fish had a long silvery rainbow-coloured body that refracted the light. Pinky didn't recognise the fish, but he said, "Hello there," nevertheless. Pinky was such a friendly sort.

This fish answered right back. "Hello there to you," the winsome fish said. The fish took a break from his swim and vibrated in place as he gazed up at the friendly Pinky. "You look like a fish out of water!" the now worried fish said.

"It's okay," Pinky said. "I'm doing just fine up here."

"How could you be, with no water flowing through your gills?" asked the anxious fish. What the fish couldn't see yet was that Pinky was just his usual gopher self in his furry homebody. Often, when meeting Pinky for the first time, one sees themselves instead of Pinky. So it was that all this fish could see was another rainbow-coloured fish. It was a strange experience, indeed.

"Oh my!" the incredulous fish said. As the fish spoke, his gills expanded. His words broke the surface in bubbles of air. "Where I come from, if it looks like a fish and swims like a fish then it's a—"

"I know," Pinky gently interrupted, "then it's a fish. I'm only just getting used to this sort of reaction," Pinky explained, with some dismay. Pinky was still growing into his *everyanimal*-ness, so he hadn't yet learned to let folks have this moment uninterrupted—the moment when they saw themselves instead of him. "I didn't mean to worry you, do have a nice day." Pinky waved goodbye with a gentle paw as the fish, somewhat reassured, swam on his way.

Pinky had no intention to cause others to feel befuddled. It's simply that his kindness had the impact of helping others think that he was just like them. This could be very useful in helping others to truly hear whatever insight he had to share with them. It was perhaps a little sad, though, to know that if others were under the impression one was just like them, they were usually more inclined to hear with an open heart and ear.

Pinky generally appeared looking like an ordinary gopher, but at first others could only see a version of themselves. This time the fish saw a fish, of course. Next time Pinky had no idea what he would be, or to whom. But he was just beginning to see that in these fleeting moments, others learned something about their own *Me*, and this was part of the true gift an everyanimal gave.

"You look like a fish out of water!" the now worried fish said.

As Pinky pondered, a commotion broke out near his colourful furry toes, which dangled from a boulder he was sitting atop. He looked down in surprise to see two squirrels playing tug of war. Well, it wasn't tug of war, really; it was more like *tug it's mine*, and they definitely weren't *playing*. They tugged back and forth on a nutshell that hadn't been cracked.

"It's mine, mine, mine!" the big, bushy one professed.

"You are most certainly mistaken, as I had it first!" the little one chirped.

Pinky watched this unfortunate scene. *They both want their breakfast*, he thought. Though Pinky was rarely one to take sides, he offered to help solve this tricky state of affairs.

"I have an idea," Pinky said to the two.

Both squirrels looked up at him with squinched-up, determined little faces.

"Yeah right you do!" the big one declared. "Mind your own business!" Indeed, the big one sounded quite rude!

"Perhaps we *should* consider this *wise* squirrel's kind offer to help us *both* out," the little one chirped in, briefly seeing herself in Pinky.

As always, Pinky was in his gopher homebody, but neither squirrel seemed aware of this. They each thought him a squirrel family match, one of their tribe, so to speak. This time, the humble Pinky had no desire to correct the impression. Perhaps he was beginning to embrace his destiny.

"I'm sure that you both want your breakfast at some point this morning," said Pinky.

The big squirrel raised his eyebrow and the little one nodded her head. Now they were both listening, but their hands held the nutshell tight like a vice.

"You could crack the nut open and each have one bite," suggested Pinky. The squirrels' eyes met across the prize held firmly between them. They looked at each other with suspicion, and Pinky saw this. "I could count to two or three and you could both let go at the same time," Pinky offered.

Each squirrel could see Pinky's point. "But if we both let go," the big one declared, "how do we know you wouldn't catch it midair, and run off to your cache?"

"Oh, I wouldn't do that," Pinky tried to reassure them, "but I see your worry. You don't know me, so how could you tell what sort of fellow I am?"

Hmm. They all pondered, and silence fell in. A long silence. Each squirrel grew hungrier as each moment passed. *What to do, what to do,* about breakfast?

Just as they were beginning to fear they would never decide just what to do, along came a wind. It ruffled up the fur of both squirrels and left tears in their eyes, but still, they dug in their heels and held on. The wind turned into rain, and the rain turned to hail. It was becoming a storm, and still, they each clung on tight to their hope for a satisfying bite—of *breakfast,* that is.

The storm was so bad it blocked the sun out! But even still, both squirrels held on tight in the dark. It seemed as though they were cut from the same stubborn cloth. Shortly after this brief mid-morning storm, the sun peeked her way through once again, only to settle her rays on two hungry, grid-locked rodents with nothing to chew. Well, nothing to chew that they were willing to let go of so that they could chew it, that is!

Through all of this rough weather—the wind, the rain, and the hail—it was curious to see that Pinky had stayed high and dry. He watched as the wind shrugged. "Thought I'd give it a try,"

whispered the wind, just before she blew on her away. It seemed even nature was trying to help these squirrely two. After all, some say, breakfast is the most important meal of the day.

After the storm, the littlest squirrel began to shiver from the cold and the bigger one gazed over the shell of the nut with his fur sopping wet.

"What do we do now?" the little one chattered.

"I don't have a clue!" sputtered the larger squirrel. "You decide. It was you who caused this mess in the first place."

"Oh, I couldn't take credit for that," was the wee one's chattering, sarcastic reply. Needless to say, these two squirrels were stumped.

Pinky was becoming increasingly concerned for the two, who stood firm, with their breakfast in view but just out of reach. He could see them both growing weary. He could hear their tummies grumbling. *If Quizzle were here*, thought Pinky, *she'd wave breakfast right up with one tip of her wand or flick of her wing.*

Not an option today, however, as Quizzle was quite far away attending a fairy dance-around-ring. Sometimes fairies from around the world get together and dance around in rings. This sharing of energy helped recharge their magic. Even if Quizzle was aware of Pinky's desire to help out these two hungry squirrels, she couldn't interrupt a ring in flight and let down the other fairies. No, she wouldn't do that.

Pinky continued to contemplate the squirrel's situation. He admired the way they were each able to look out for themselves. *Looking out for oneself is a necessary talent if one wishes to survive*, he mused. *Yes indeed, self-provision is one way to carry on, to be sure. But then there are so many to choose from*, thought Pinky, as he studiously pushed his glasses back up to the bridge of his nose.

Perched upon his rock by the watery pool, Pinky began to consider what the squirrels' best option could be in this particular moment, and how he could be of most help on this particular day. After some careful consideration, he decided that his next step should be to get to know these squirrels a little better. After all, they'd only just met. Pinky needed to get a handle on each one's point of view before he put in his two cents. *Yes indeed, it was the only fair thing to do. One can't go around helping others solve their problems until one has taken a walk in their paws*, Pinky thought.

From up on his rock, Pinky was a little above the heads of these two feisty squirrels. He decided it best if they met on the same level ground, so he stepped himself down, ever so slowly, and sat himself a little closer. The squirrels watched with interest, and perhaps with a little curiosity, too. After all, they had never before seen a multicoloured squirrel. As usually happened after a while, Pinky was beginning to look less like a squirrel and more like himself to these two. However, the squirrels were not at all aware of everyanimals and what they could do to help others get on.

Pinky's fur had been changing colour as he contemplated the whole situation, and this changing of colour had begun to distract these two squirrels, just a wee bit. At this moment Pinky's fur was vibrating in hues of light blues and soft yellows. Truly, he presented as such an affable dude, indeed, the dude that he was. But to them, he began to seem like a magical squirrel.

Pinky decided to ask them each a question. Then he thought ever so carefully about which question to choose. When he had his question in mind, he turned to the big one and said, "What's it like to be you?"

Still holding on tight to his possible breakfast, but turning slightly in Pinky's direction, the big one said, "Hmm," but resisted scratching his head. "Well, in this moment, I must admit, I have run out of wit." The larger squirrel had somewhat softened his tone. He really looked spent.

Then Pinky turned to the littler one and asked, "What's it like to be you?" "W-*w-well*," the little one chattered, still freezing cold and wet from the storm, "I *cou-cou-cou-could* use a bit of a break to *bl-bl-blow* my nose, and I am very *f-f-f-froze*," she sputtered, ignoring her grammar. She was beginning to look quite frail.

Pinky looked back at the bigger squirrel, just to check in.

The bigger squirrel sighed a big sigh as he began to see the little one's plight, made all the more obvious by the snot that ran down her nose. In that moment, the moment he looked, his thoughts were for *her*, and now he was hooked! *Darn, she did it to me again!* he thought with a little regret, but not too much. "Okay, sis. You put down your end and I'll take a break. Go blow your nose. I'll stay put and wait," he said somewhat begrudgingly.

"Oh, thank you, big brother," the little one said with relief.

Pinky felt a little relief, too. He watched as the smaller squirrel gently let go of her end. Now her two hands were free! Then she reached deep into her pocket to pull out her hanky. She stepped away a little, just to be polite. Then she blew and she blew. When she was all done, she folded her hanky up, just as she was taught to do, and placed it back in her pocket for safekeeping. Then she walked back to her end of the nut and picked up, exactly where she had left off! One might just wonder if that could have been a missed opportunity? Hmm.

"It's mine," the little sister said as she resumed with a tug.

"No, I had it first," the big brother declared, and he tugged it right back.

Pinky smiled a slow soft smile. He watched now with some amusement as these siblings carried on with their song and their dance. At this point, "Mine, mine, mine!" was all they could hear, so Pinky waited patiently for his next opportunity to lend a paw or bend an ear.

By-and-by, after several tugs and an equal number of pulls, the siblings grew tired yet again. They each stopped to catch their breath, but still with their tiny fingers and thumbs gripping the nutshell. While they huffed and they puffed, Pinky asked softly, and most sincerely, "Is it time for breakfast *yet*?"

Pinky pondered, *Hmm*, and then Pinky thought, *Well it seems they are each caught up in one point of view, and for each, it's their own.* Pinky sighed a big sigh. As he watched the *tug-it's-mine* crew, he looked this way and that, and this way and that. He may as well have been watching a game of ping pong, but no one had yet scored a single point. Pinky felt caught up in a jam! He sighed another big sigh.

Pinky was becoming overwhelmed and very confused as his squirrel friends tugged, it seemed, with no end, back and forth and back and forth. Pinky stood up and started pacing, back and forth and back and forth, too. Pinky had a lot to process!

To understand this turn of events, one would have to take a walk in his paws. One would have to imagine what it was like to be Pinky in this moment. He had spent much of his morning trying to help out two squirrels who thought him kin but refused to give in. Earlier on, a fish had become upset thinking he was a fish out of water, but to himself, he was just his *Me*. Since Quizzle was out of town, for him there was no one around; well, no one around who knew who he had been, or was, or wanted to be. This was a lot to bear for such a young everyanimal. He couldn't even tell if things were moving too fast or going too slow. Despite his best efforts, it all seemed the same! Back and forth and back and forth went this *tug-it's-mine* game.

It was time for Pinky to take a very deep breath and calm himself down. Pinky put his paw on his belly and breathed in very slowly through his nose and released each breath through his mouth. In through his nose, and out through his mouth. Then, ever so slowly, he did it again and again. Pinky gradually began to calm down. He thought about being an everyanimal. He knew this was something that enhanced with time, like most good things. He had also been taught by his elders that becoming a fully evolved everyanimal was an inside job, so to speak. Oh, sure, it could shine through all right, but Pinky knew this was not about changing on the outside; this was more about fine-tuning what happened on the inside. Pinky was going through a transformation, indeed!

As one may remember, the most important thing about being an everyanimal, was caring for others. *Well sometimes*, thought Pinky, *caring for others is harder than it looks.*

"What about me?" Pinky spoke softly to himself. Pinky had a longing; a longing to be seen! It seemed that every time he opened his heart up to care for another, they thought he was just like them. It was true that with Pinky, others could feel seen and heard and cared for in such a warm way that they confused his *Me* for their *Me*. Sometimes for others, Pinky wasn't a *they*. Instead, they were all one. *This is so complicated*, thought Pinky. *I just have to get out of my own way!*

"Easy to say!" some would declare, but getting out of one's own way is perhaps the hardest thing in the world to do! Pinky, however, was still very new. What he had yet to learn was that it doesn't *all* have to happen in *one* day. Pinky took another deep breath and gazed around with tears in his eyes. He was beginning to feel like he really was a "fish out of water."

Pinky looked softly through his tears at the squirrels. Then he chuckled a warm chuckle when he noticed the *tug-it's-mine* crew. They had each caught their breath and stood ready to answer Pinky's earlier question.

"Yes, it's time now," the littlest squirrel said to Pinky.

"Time for breakfast," the big one agreed.

The two siblings nodded to each other and slowly loosened their grip as their tummies gurgled in sync. They set down their breakfast and then with a great big stomp and a well-placed chop, they cracked the nutshell right there on the ground! When the shell cracked open, they discovered that there were two, two nuts inside! Oh my, and they had tugged for such a long time.

"What changed your minds?" Pinky asked the *tug-it's-mine* crew, as they each ate their breakfast in haste with barely enough time to taste.

"Well," said the big brother between chomps, "I must say, I was getting so hungry!"

"Me too, me too!" echoed the little sister squirrel, "me too."

"We just thought we'd try something new," they chanted in unison.

In fact, when one has tried to solve a problem the same way, over and over and over again (which many before have done), it's always a good clue to try something new.

Smiling at his well-nourished friends, Pinky prepared to head his own way. Breakfast was fun. But lunchtime was near, and Pinky needed a break. He'd been given much 'food for thought' on this day, and he had bitten off as much as he could possibly chew. But of one thing he was sure—his tummy could use a bite, too!

The Care and Feeding of a Guardian Angel

One by one the brightly coloured red, orange, and brown leaves gently surrendered their grip on summer. Spinning and falling freely, they laughed and giggled their way to the forest floor. Fall had arrived in Tree Forest and the little town of Justaroundthebend.

Quizzle and her little angel—to whom she had given the name Titania—sat in Pinky's rock garden, sipping lemonade and playing games. The little angel squealed with glee as she won her turn. Pinky sat nearby, turning the pages of the *Guardian Angel Training Manual*. He had to keep pushing up his glasses, as they kept sliding down his nose. When he got to the part on how to make an angel behave, he increased his concentration. After the big chase scene at Quizzle's flying up party, Pinky had been trying to get this part down pat.

Guardian angels can be such complicated little creatures, he thought.

Then moments later, "Oh, I see!" the serious Pinky said out loud, more to himself than to anyone else. "They come with a whistle."

The lavender-haired angel looked up from her game. She sneaked a peek at Pinky out of one corner of her eye as she fondled a decorative chain she wore around her neck. Pinky didn't know this, but the clever little angel had concealed her whistle by hanging it on the chain around her neck and tucking it into her dress. Engraved on the whistle, which no one could see, were the words: *Just Whistle and I'll Be There*. While this inscription was true, it was also a fact that the little angel didn't at all like to be told what to do. That was why she chose to keep this whistle out of view, at least for the time being.

Where is that whistle? Pinky thought. *Perhaps it's in the box she came in?* Pinky pushed up his glasses once again and went inside his burrow to have a look around. It wasn't in her box. He walked up one tunnel and down the next, searching for her whistle. *Where could it be? Where could it be?* he wondered. By the time Quizzle and Titania had come in from their game, Pinky had turned the whole burrow upside down.

"What are you looking for?" Quizzle asked Pinky.

"They come with a whistle," he whistled.

"And so do you," giggled Quizzle.

Pinky and the guardian angel chuckled, too, each in their own way. Titania was enjoying her new charges immensely, and today was a very special day. The search for the whistle—which wasn't really lost—would have to wait, because it was Halloween, and Quizzle had promised Titania she would teach her all about this very special day.

Titania had heard about Halloween, and although she'd never been trick-or-treating, Quizzle had been telling her all about it. Titania had a sweet tooth and could almost taste the candy of which she dreamt. They had all planned to go out together after dark, but dark was a long time away and there was still much to do. They had to decide on their costumes for one thing, and for another, they still had to weave baskets to hold the candy they would receive. Then they had to make a jack-o'-lantern, which is a carved-out pumpkin with a light inside. The pumpkins didn't mind; in fact, they waited for this all summer, trying to grow as big and fat as they could. Every year there was a prize awarded to the biggest pumpkin, and each one wanted to win.

Titania was going as a little devil, surprise, surprise! She had a costume with a pitchfork and everything. She and Quizzle had sewn a red cloak using glowing thread, and they fashioned a pitchfork out of things they found lying around in the shed. On her head, Titania wore two little horns that glowed in the dark, and from under her cloak protruded a pointy tail. The whole ensemble was simply to die for! Who would ever suspect that on All Hallows Eve an angel would come disguised as a little devil? Could what they say be true, that there's a little devil in everyone?

Pinky wore a golden crown. He was dressed up as a frog prince just waiting for a kiss. Quizzle dressed up as a cowgirl, lasso and all. What a trio they were!

What Quizzle, Pinky, and Titania couldn't know was that Wag was coming, and that was no tale. Wag was a tall, skinny witch, skin and bone some would say. When she turned sideways, she seemed to almost slip away. Wag was a real witch—and not the good kind, at least not anymore. Wag's toes curled with rage, and she smelled nothing like sage, though she slinked around in a smoky haze. She was mean, and she was smart. She could trick the skin off a snake's back. Well, actually, snakes are always shedding their skin, but Wag took credit for it anyway. She was not an honest sort.

Wag could lie her way out of any kind of mess she was able to create. The thing about a good lie, she understood, was that it had to be surrounded by truth so no one would know that a lie had been told. Wag was coming, and she was mad.

Wag was out to get that *stuck up little fairy* who hadn't invited her to the flying up party. Of all parties *not* to be invited to, not to be invited to a *flying up party* was the biggest insult to a witch with a fast broom!

If Quizzle were to ever need a guardian angel, with Wag on her way, tonight would be the night.

Halloween in Justaroundthebend was a magical event that the whole town and all the surrounding forest creatures, including the forest itself, looked forward to with great anticipation. Dragonfly and Hummingbird were going as little gnats, and Skunk would dress up as a sweet, cuddly house cat. Millie Mole wore a little tiger suit that she'd been saving in her bottom drawer. She would go door to door with Ricky Rabbit, who would be dressed in a very tall hat that he refused to jump out of for once. The woods were alive with the sounds of snipping, carving, and... cackling? One might well guess who was doing the cackling!

Anyone who has ever gone for a walk in the woods during the fall can imagine the sights and sounds, and the wispy smell of smoke in the air. The autumn leaves melted into the landscape, preparing their winter beds. Nearing dusk on that particular day, the air was cool and moist with a hint of musk, too. All was ready when, without a moment to spare, from across the forest Wag tipped her wicked broom into the cool night air. Wag loved Halloween! This was her chance to travel unseen; with so many fake witches milling about it was hard to tell just who the real witches were. Wag waited all year for this element of surprise, and she was truly intent on Quizzle's demise.

Pinky, Quizzle, and Titania made their way into town by way of a forest path. Titania rode on Quizzle's shoulder, as guardian angels are wont to do. On this particular night, however, it appeared that Quizzle had a little devil on her shoulder.

The forest was afloat with ghouls, goblins, and ghosts. The woods echoed with peels of laughter and squeals of fright as the tricksters started to play. Jack-o'-lanterns lit the way, and some told ghost stories to frighten passersby. Yes, these pumpkins could talk! In fact, some of them were so bold that they never shut up.

Stepping ever so gingerly past these yappy pumpkins was one nervous yellow dog. Mrs. Grupple remembered that she had a pumpkin stuck on her head during her first meeting with Quizzle and her friends. She had no intention of repeating that scary experience, and was doing everything she could to not be noticed by these boastful pumpkins. When Grupple saw Quizzle, Pinky, and Titania coming, she wagged her happy tail and joined in with her friends. Together, they carried on down the trail.

That Halloween night there were so many scary sounds that it was difficult to tell one from the other. Set apart from other sounds, though, was one wicked cackle that could send a shiver up the bravest spine. Pinky, Quizzle, Titania, and Grupple stopped in their tracks as the alarming cackle grew near and then faded into the distance. Mrs. Grupple's usually floppy ears stuck straight up in the air.

"What was that?" Pinky whistled. His usual bravery escaped him momentarily as shivers went up his spine.

"I don't know, but it sounds so real!" said Quizzle. Titania got nervous and started to shake. "Hold on tight, my little angel," whispered Quizzle. They all shook the fear out of their heads and carried on.

Further along the path they ran into Skunk, who meowed like a cat.

"Hi Skunk," Quizzle said.

"How did you know it was me?" Skunk asked. As they went past, Pinky pointed at Skunk's sneaky little black and white tail; it had wiggled its way out of her costume, so now it looked like Skunk had two tails.

Next, they came upon Millie and Ricky. Millie was the smallest tiger any of them had ever seen, and she was being very careful not to get under foot. Ricky looked regal in his tall, tall, top hat, with a little tiger on his arm. Finally, floating along as though in a dream, came Auntie Hoolahoop; although she was a hundred and two in fairy years, she had yet to miss a single Halloween. Auntie Hoolahoop wore a hundred and two veils that glowed in the dark.

"Hello my dears," Auntie Hoolahoop whispered as she continued her flight. The trees stood bathed in eerie moonlight, their branches waving in the breeze. Off in the distance wolves howled, a chilling sound until you got to know them. The shadows of all the trick-or-treaters danced on the rocks and on the trunks of some trees. It was as if the rocks and the trees had a life of their own. My goodness, by now we know that they did!

Quizzle, Pinky, Titania, and their friends stumbled through the dark, chilling woods and eventually poured into the town square. The little village of Justaroundthebend was alight with Jack-o'-lanterns and glow-in-the-dark pictures of the Town Council, who never missed a photo opportunity. Woven around all of the lamp posts were bright green webs sparkling with spiders, and all the park benches skipped around freely, offering themselves to anyone who might need a rest. In the center of the square was a great big tank brimming with bums, or so it looked, as many of the town's folk were bobbing for apples. There were bums with tails and bums with patches and bums dressed in brightly coloured garb. Occasionally, a head would appear with a splash and a gasp, before disappearing again, bum up. Quizzle, Pinky, and the little angel-devil had never seen so many of their neighbours upside down in one place. They couldn't help but laugh loud and long when Judge Justapeek lost his footing and ended up all wet in the tub!

Amid this merriment, however, was one who was not so merry. Wag only pretended to clean up the mess with her broom as she skulked around looking for the *stuck up little fairy*. The wicked Wag was after Quizzle's wings! Now we all know witches fly on brooms and not with wings, but this was not necessarily by choice. When witches finally started to fly, brooms were all they had left. This is not to say Wag couldn't fly 'round the moon; she was quite good with her broom.

Wag carried a pair of brand-new *wing removers* in her pocket and couldn't wait to use them. Perhaps Quizzle had met her match—or had Wag met hers? It was far too early to tell. One thing seemed clear, however: Wag was all on her own. This is not to say she didn't have friends. Wag's 'friends' were all out of town, so to speak. They had *this and that* to do.

Upside down or bum side up?

Wag had a difficult childhood, but we won't go there. Suffice it to say, she had never been allowed to play, and this goes a long way to explaining how she turned out so mean and so rotten. Rotten to the core she was, and there was no going back. What the villagers hadn't noticed was that Wag's broom was no ordinary broom: it was 'loaded.' Tied to its back was a little fairy-catcher made out of net. Having located her prey, Wag was waiting for the right moment. She knew it was not wise to strike in a crowd. She would bide her wicked time and wait until Quizzle was all alone in the dark.

The trick-or-treaters began to gather in groups as the grand prize for the largest pumpkin was announced. The winner rolled 'round the town square in delight. But Titania, with her sweet tooth, couldn't wait to get going and get some loot, so the foursome, including Mrs. Grupple, all headed off to another part of town.

Mrs. Grupple waited at the curb, knowing full-well that candy is not good for dogs, while Pinky, Quizzle, and their little angel in disguise arrived at the first door and rang the bell. "Trick or treat!" they called, noticing a flickering flame from within as slow shadows slipped along the inside walls. Titania's little eyes were wide with wonder and anticipation as the creaky door opened.

When old Mr. Salamander opened the door, he couldn't help but admire the handsome young Salamander standing before him! Or was this a frog prince?

He was so sure he had seen him somewhere before! Pinky, Quizzle, and Titania stood before him. Their baskets awaited. The kindly old Mr. Salamander shook the confusion out of his head, reached into his bucket teaming with treats, and pulled out three gooey gobs. He placed one in each of their waiting baskets and said, "Happy Halloween!" to the trio, just as a new mob of pranksters arrived on the porch. They had all heard Mr. Salamander was handing out home-made gooey gobs this year.

Soon the friends came to the next abode, and out from within popped Mr. Willy Weasel doing his Halloween dance. His basket was brimming with *jumble* and *chance*. Titania snapped up a red one, and Quizzle picked a blue; then Pinky chose a green one, and off they went to the next home.

The trio made so many stops that their baskets were full, or at least they should have been full. When Quizzle and Pinky stopped under a lamppost to examine their loot, they peered into the little angel's basket and found only one treat left. Titania smiled up at them, with a chocolaty grin, rubbing her tummy with chagrin. The guardian angel didn't feel so well, and no one wondered why. With a sigh, they decided to head home for the night.

As Quizzle, Pinky, Mrs. Grupple, and Titania made their way back up the forest path, guess who stopped by? Well, she didn't *stop* by; actually, she *whooshed* by, wielding a fairy catcher and wearing a wicked grin. Wag's cackle sliced through the dark as she whooshed by again and again.

"You stuck up little fairy!" she chanted. "I'll catch you!"

Quizzle, Pinky, and all the surrounding creatures were frozen with fright, and Wag was counting on this. But one creature wasn't frozen! Despite her bloated belly, Quizzle's guardian angel kept her wits about her. She reached into her little devil costume, pulled her whistle out of concealment, and pressed it firmly into Quizzle's little hand.

"Just whistle and I'll be there," she whispered into the beautiful fairy's ear.

Then Pinky shook off his fright, and realizing this was no game, ripped off his costume and began leaping up in the air, pumping his fists like a real boxer. He was going to knock that hag right off of her broom if she didn't change her tune. Mrs. Grupple barked and leapt up at the broom, but all she managed to sink her teeth into was air. Suddenly, Quizzle and Titania were gone! Wag was gone! There was no one there. There was nothing but air. Pinky turned all blue. He didn't know what to do. A single tear rolled down his furry face as he stared with disbelief up into the cold (now silent) night sky. Mrs. Grupple nudged him with her wet nose, letting him know he wasn't alone.

Thankfully, from out of the woods stepped one friend after another. Mrs. Grupple's fierce bark and the stark silence had drawn them near. They gathered together out of concern for their dear little Quizzle. The whole town of Justaroundthebend and the surrounding area put their heads together, and with a whisper and a whir, a harrumph and a buzz, a song and a dance, a prayer and a chant, and a mumble and grumble, they all realized that they hadn't a clue about what to do.

"Where does the witch live?" someone piped up.

"She didn't leave her address," Pinky spat out as his fur turned red. He was furious!

"We need to find out," spoke up another.

"I once heard tell she lived in a cave," someone said.

"A cave?" Pinky repeated as he pulled out his map. Pinky was always very good at reading maps.

"I know every cave and tunnel in this whole area!" he said. The town's folk sighed. They were quiet little sighs, the kind one makes when hope is uncertain. They took turns peering over Pinky's shoulder at the map.

Quizzle and her guardian angel were far, far away, and neither knew where. It was damp where they sat, all clammy and cold. They both chilled with fright every time Wag's cackle echoed through the cavernous cave. Fear was an element Wag understood very well; in fact, one might say she counted on it. Fear was her fuel.

"If music be the food of love," as someone once said, "then fear be the food of evil witches."

Wag cackled and peered down the long tunnel at her *dear* little *friends*. With every cackle from Wag, and every shiver and shake from Quizzle and Titania, Wag grew larger. A bright, hungry fire burned inside her, full of jealousy and envy. Her long, pointy red fingers reached out from beneath her cape. Her toes curled and smoked. Her evil eyes were cold as steel on a winter's day. She had been waiting for this moment, and she hated to wait. This was her moment, all hers! Not a drop of kindness hung in the air.

The town's folk hustled and bustled, running up and flying down as Pinky called out for supplies. They had to find all the equipment they would need. They gathered shovels and ladders and hats with lights. There were ropes and pulleys and clamps, all of which they carried in their pouches and strapped to their backs. They were ready!

Pinky had looked and looked and looked at his map until he estimated just where his Quizzle would be. Mrs. Grupple, who dearly loved Quizzle, too, sniffed at the map and peered hopefully over Pinky's shoulder. There was one dark tunnel he'd never gone down, and he was sure that this was the home of the witch. He was sure, because one day when he was a wee one at play, he had fallen into a ditch and thought he'd spied a witch. When he told his parents, they warned him not to go that way again. He had forgotten that episode until now. It was as if the whole terrible experience had been temporarily erased from his memory. But now he could remember the bones at the mouth of her cave and the spooky sounds of screaming, pleading, and crying echoing from inside.

"We have to move fast!" he called to his crew, and they all followed Pinky. They scrambled through bramble and scurried up cliffs. They paddled the lake and the rapids so wild. They leapt over gorges and valleys and streams. The little town of Justaroundthebend was determined to win, and they were just about there.

Just about might be a moment too late! For what seemed like forever now, Wag had swaggered her way around. She had slowly grown bigger and bigger with each step. She fed off each fear that crossed the poor worried minds of Quizzle and her angel. Suddenly, Quizzle remembered the whistle her angel had so willingly given her. *What good can this be with my angel so near?* she wondered.

Just as she was about to blow the whistle to see what might happen, a light appeared at the end of the tunnel. The light moved closer and closer, but so did the witch.

The light better hurry up, thought Quizzle. She and Titania looked to the light and they surrendered their fear. Their faith increased as the light came closer. As their faith grew, the wicked witch began to shrink.

Wag was waning.

Now those of you who have ever seen miners heading down the shafts for the day may recall the lights on their hats. The whole town wore hats with lights as they crawled down the tunnel towards Quizzle and Titania, with a very brave yellow dog in front sniffing out the way. They had been driven by love, the love of a friend! Wag let out one long, lonely cackle. There was no fear left for her to feed on since her cave was now filled with love.

Yuck, she thought, and poof, she went. She couldn't stand to be around so much love.

One may ask, what does this all have to do with the training of a guardian angel?

Quizzle gently pressed the whistle back into her guardian angel's hand. "They don't have to come when you whistle," she said softly to herself, "they're already there when you need them."

Quizzle looked up at the many shining faces of her friends. *In fact*, she thought, *I'm surrounded by angels!*

Pinky's Wish

Pinky burrowed his way through the deep snow as he headed into town to do his Christmas shopping. The small woodland village sparkled with lights. Christmas was just around the corner in Justaroundthebend. Mr. Penny, a kindly aardvark and the town's shopkeeper, was very busy with his customers. They wanted all sorts of goodies! They wanted chocolate truffles and candy canes. They wanted ice skates and little toy trains. They wanted pop-ups and cut-outs. They wanted storybooks and games. They wanted mittens and gloves and little toy bugs. They wanted... well, there was no end to what they wanted. What they wanted, however, and what they could afford were often two separate things.

Pinky stopped for a moment to catch his breath and gazed longingly up at the sky. As always, he was looking for Quizzle, or even faint, sparkly traces of where she may have been on this snowy afternoon. *If I could just spot where she's been*, Pinky surmised, *this could be a clue as to where she might land*. But Quizzle had had no time to touch down, no time for feet on the ground, and Pinky couldn't fly up to the sky. Christmas eve was a hectic time for fairies, and the industrious Quizzle had been out making wishes come true since dawn! Could she have forgotten just one?

Pinky blinked as a snowflake floated by, catching a sparkle of light. He missed Quizzle so much that every sparkle reminded him of his dear friend. "Oh well," he said to himself. "I'm sure she'll find time to fly by." He sighed a big sigh.

In the heart of town Mr. Penny's shop door jingled with bells, and in came little Old Lady Muskrat wearing a torn hat. She was an odd sort of creature, not a coin in hand, and she looked quite chilled. "Good day," said Mr. Penny, who was always polite.

"Good day," she said back. "I've just come in for the warmth..." she hesitated.... "If you don't mind?"

"Not at all, my dear, not at all, yes do come in." Mr. Penny ushered her over to a rocking chair by the wood stove, which she accepted with grace. Not all shopkeepers are a miserly sort, and Mr. Penny was both generous and kind. Some would say he was too generous, that this could be bad for his bottom line—his count at the end of the day, so to speak.

Old Lady Muskrat rocked in her chair as she slowly sipped the cup of steaming hot tea Mr. Penny had poured her. She was very cold and really quite sad, but she was too proud to talk about it. She was all alone this Christmas, having barely enough to eat; but at least her toes were warming up, and now she had a good cup of tea in her paw. She watched as the customers looked at *this* and rattled *that*. *What a pleasant scene*, she thought, as she sipped and rocked and rocked and sipped. She thought of all the Christmas days she'd known, and there had been quite a few very pleasant ones.

The jingle bell door opened again and again as more villagers entered, searching for the gifts they would give. From where she sat, Old Lady Muskrat could see what everyone was giving (and getting, too). She could imagine the joy on the sweet little faces of the youngsters who would open these gifts on Christmas morning. The store was abustle with beavers and squirrels, elves and dwarfs, rabbits and moles and dear little pocket mice. It was a very diverse and colourful crowd, but there were no fairies.

Fairies, one should understand, don't celebrate Christmas—not in the usual way. Many have heard the story of how sugar plum fairies dance in the heads of little children on Christmas Eve, which is not an easy job with so many heads and so few fairies. Surely, anyone who has lost a tooth is also aware of tooth fairies and what they do. Then there are the fairy godmothers and fairy princesses, garden fairies, and forest fairies, too. Fairies, in fact, are a hard-working lot, and when there's magic afoot, they're right on the spot.

Today, however, there was not a fairy to be seen. This is not to say they weren't there; it's just that they couldn't be seen. Today, all the fairies in Justaroundthebend, and all around the world for that matter, were on secret missions making wishes come true. Sure enough, there *was* a fairy in the store, but who knows where?

Wishes bestowed by fairies are not about presents. Santa takes care of that. The wishes fairies grant are wishes from the heart. Oh, sure, there are other kinds of wishes, including party wishes and such, but on Christmas, fairies like to focus all their magic on making wishes from the heart come true. "What is a wish from the heart?" one might ask. "How can someone be sure a wish from the heart is not a wish from somewhere else?"

Wishes from the heart are *sacred wishes*. A wish from the heart is something one actually feels in the heart. Sometimes they hurt with a pang, and when these wishes come true, the heart expands to make room for all the joy and blessings they bring.

Someone in the store had a wish, a wish that was waning, and that was not a good thing. A waning wish is a sad thing to behold. It can happen when one loses hope that the wish will come true. A waning wish fades ever so slowly; so slowly, in fact, that sometimes not even the one who dreamt up the wish in the first-place notices when it's gone. A wish is like a dream, and what they say about dreams is true: *Hold on to them, but not too tight.* Wishes need room to breathe. When we speak of real wishes, they're not of the idle kind. A really good wish requires a certain focus, a powerful intention. Behind every good wish from the heart is the ability to accept things just as they are. Not an easy thing to do by any means!

The jingle bell door jingled again and in came Pinky, shaking the snow from his paws.

"Hello, Pinky, my boy," Mr. Penny chuckled, happy to see his young friend. "Come right in. Come right in," he said twice. Mr. Penny had a slight penchant for repeating himself.

"Hi, Mr. Penny," Pinky whistled. Pinky was looking for a present. The coins he'd been saving jingled in his pocket. He wanted to get something nice to put under Quizzle's tree. But what Pinky didn't know was that Quizzle had no tree. Well, not a *Christmas* tree, to be specific. Her fairy hive hung from an oak tree, but this was an all-year-round, stuck in the ground sort of tree.

Pinky looked here and there. As Pinky was looking, he noticed something strange. Off in a corner, at the back of the store, sat a rat nibbling some cheese; but that wasn't the strange part. Next to the rat sat a hat that was far too big for the rat; but that, too, wasn't unusual. It probably wasn't even the rat's hat. Perhaps it belonged to some cat. What was strange and unusual was a tiny *sparkle-and-glint* of light that quickly disappeared. It was this bit of dancing light that had caught Pinky's eye.

What was that? he wondered as he made his way to the back of the store to investigate.

Pinky was an ever-curious sort of fellow. Every bit of this and every bit of that was of interest to Pinky. This particular sparkle-and-glint, however, was having a special effect on him. As he gazed around, he saw it again!

There it is! he thought. *My eyes haven't been fooling me!* Pinky's eyes had never fooled him once, and so, for Pinky to think his eyes had betrayed him was an illogical thought. His eyes blinked and blinked again until Pinky got them back into focus.

The sparkle-and-glint was just the tiniest speck, but it seemed to be animated. It danced over here and flitted over there with great determination. Pinky watched through scrunched up eyes, trying to get a more focused view. He decided to wait until whatever it was landed. He waited a bit, and sure enough, the speck settled itself on the windowsill.

Pinky slowly and carefully made his way over, not wanting to scare off the speck. As he came closer, he began to realize that whatever he was watching was more than a speck: it was a bubble! Looking very closely, he could even see that the bubble contained something. Pinky reached into his warm winter coat, pulled out his magnifying glass, and looked again. Inside the bubble was a word: HELP!

Oh my, what could this mean? he asked himself. *Where could this message in a bubble have come from?*

Pinky was puzzled. He began to think about bubbles. He thought of all the places bubbles could come from: one could find bubbles in one's bath, resting on the rim of a milkshake glass, gathered at the edge of a stream, or bursting out of a bottle of pop. There were just so many! Pinky's tummy gurgled.

Next, he thought about how bubbles were made. There was always some sort of liquid or slime involved, and all bubbles were full of air. This particular bubble looked very much like a soap bubble. Pinky thought of bursting the bubble with the pin on some hat, but Pinky was too kind for that. Then he decided to use his own words.

"Help who?" Pinky whistled. The bubble seemed to change colours, and then there was a commotion inside.

"Me," came the answer.

"Who is Me?" asked Pinky.

"I," said the bubble—or the creature inside.

Pinky began to think this bubble was trouble. He maintained his patience. "Who is I?" he asked.

"You," came the answer. Now Pinky was very confused!

Some of the shoppers had noticed Pinky, and a few of them were concerned that he'd gone mad. Who could blame them, though, for this is what they saw: Pinky at the back of the store, standing next to a rat nibbling some cheese near a hat, talking to himself as he looked through a magnifying glass. Mr. Penny nodded to his concerned customers and walked over to Pinky.

"Who are you speaking with?" asked Mr. Penny ever so confidentially.

Pinky looked up at Mr. Penny with a magnified eye.

"Well, Mr. Penny," he whistled, "it would appear I've been talking to myself."

"Fascinating, fascinating my boy!" said Mr. Penny with extra politeness.

Pinky knew what Mr. Penny was thinking. "No, no," he explained, "something in the bubble said, *it's me* and that *I* need *HELP*."

"What's in the bubble?" Mr. Penny asked.

"Me," Pinky whistled, "me!"

"Oh, my dear boy," said Mr. Penny. "We'll have to get you out right away!" Then he added, "You must have a chill, Pinky; come and sit by my stove."

The frustrated and confused Pinky allowed himself to be gently guided over to the warm stove. Mr. Penny placed a steaming cup in his paw; Pinky sipped and shook his head and sipped and shook his head some more. Old Lady Muskrat looked knowingly at Pinky. Her eyes seemed to say: *I know. I know.* Perhaps she did. Elders can be very wise.

Old Lady Muskrat and Pinky put their heads together, pondering Pinky's plight. "Well, you'll just have to *find* yourself," Old Lady Muskrat said. Pinky instinctively knew she was right; but first, he wanted to buy a present for Quizzle. The store would be closing soon, and tonight was Christmas Eve.

Pinky stood on his hind paws and headed once again towards the back of the store, not far from the place he had been before. He looked at this and gently touched that, but before long, the bubble was back! The bubble tumbled in the air and settled softly on Pinky's nose. Inside the bubble there were no more words, just moving pictures. Pinky seemed to be hypnotised as he gazed inside. What he thought he saw was a *bird's-eye view*. This came with a strange soaring sensation. Then off the bubble blew! *What could this message in a bubble mean?* Pinky wondered.

Pinky looked up at Mr. Penny with a magnified eye.

Overcome by self consciousness, he quickly looked around. Everyone in the store was doing their own thing. Mr. Penny was completing a sale at his cash register, and Old Lady Muskrat had nodded off in her chair. Pinky was relieved not to be met with any other inquisitive stares.

After some more shopping, Pinky was finally able to make his purchase, and then he stepped out into the snow. He tucked Quizzle's gift into his coat and stuffed his paws deep into his pockets, as it was ever so cold. There was not a penny left in his pocket, but there was still the sacred wish! As some may recall, this special wish had been given to him by his dear friend Quizzle just before she flew up to become a fully-fledged fairy. He'd been carrying it around for months and he still hadn't used it. At times he had been so distracted by his adventures that he had forgotten the wish all together. The truth is, Quizzle had noticed this, but a fully-fledged fairy is not allowed to point out an unused wish once it has been tendered. Fairies are taught to wait patiently until each recipient chooses what to wish for in their own special time.

Although Pinky was an *everyanimal* and cared deeply for everyone and everything, he was in the habit of forgetting just one: himself. He had forgotten his *Me*! Now this kind of forgetting is just not okay. A forgotten *Me* leaves dear friends at bay. After all, it takes two *Me*'s to play.

"Ahh!" he declared out loud to himself, "That's it!" *Maybe that message in a bubble wasn't trouble*, he thought. *Maybe it was a reminder to remember me? Hmm, but a reminder to remember what about me?* he wondered.

Pinky rubbed the shiny blue gem in his pocket. This sacred wish had waited patiently for what seemed like a very long time. There were just so many wishes he could make. "Perhaps I should use it to find myself?" Pinky said out loud as he trudged through the snow. "But that could be a waste of a perfectly good wish, because for all intents and purposes, here I am!" Pinky talked himself all the way up the road, although he would have much rather been chatting with his sparkly friend by his side. Could Pinky finally be getting ready to make his wish?

Back inside the store, Mr. Penny was completing his penny count for the day. "One, two, three, four..." and Old Lady Muskrat was heading for the door.

"Thank you, Mr. Penny," she offered as she jingled the jingle bell door. And then Old Lady Muskrat stepped into the night to make her way home in the dark. She did have a wish this Christmas, although as one may have guessed, it was *her* wish that was waning. She wanted to see her beloved children; but her children were grownups now and lived far away, and she was ever so near.

"Oh me..." she sighed to herself. "I truly wish my loves were here." Just as Old Lady Muskrat spoke her frail and lonely wish, the tiniest spark of hope lit in her eye...but then it turned into a tear and rolled down her cheek. Oh well, she thought as she watched her tear drop away and disappear into the snow. *I don't want to be a bother.*

Now, whenever there's a sparkle-and-glint nearby, remember, one is never alone in the dark. Inside Old Lady Muskrat's tear was a fairy on a secret mission, and a determined little fairy at that! Quizzle shook the salty tear from her wing before it could freeze. Old Lady Muskrat's family was quite far away. This mission could take up the rest of Quizzle's Christmas eve day! Off she flew to see just what she could do.

Now Old Lady Muskrat was a noble sort. She and her dear husband had truly enjoyed helping their little ones grow up to be good and kind. When it was time for them to leave home, she wore a very brave face. After her kits had moved on, she was content to stay with her dear husband, George. For many years they made their way, until even George could no longer stay. Sadly, it was George's time to slip away. When George died, her burrow felt bare. Her *Me* just wasn't enough without someone else there!

What Old Lady Muskrat didn't know was that, although far away, her offspring were thinking of her, too. Her grownup children had burrowed in for the day and were whispering sweet childhood memories to their own little kits in the dark. They shared sweet memories of the time their dear mom and dad lit up the pond on Christmas eve night, a magical delight. It was just then that they heard someone giggle, and a little one spotted a spark in the dark! In Quizzle flew to this whispering brood. "Come with me," she whispered as she caught her breath. "Come for a ride!"

Now this crew had an adventuresome side. Into the snowy night they did glide, with Quizzle as guide. But where did they go in all this snow?

Old Lady Muskrat was back at home and tucked into bed for the night when suddenly she woke up to a knock at the door. "Oh, my goodness!" she said when she saw who was there. There were twelve Muskrats standing on her front step, and they all carried gifts. There were her grown children, and some little kits, too, whom she hadn't yet met.

"Merry Christmas, Grandma!" a little one said. As they all came inside, her home was filled with cheer, and with what they unpacked, her cupboards would be full for a year!

Back at home now, Pinky sat with his mom and his pop as he revealed his beautiful present for Quizzle. Pinky had chosen Quizzle a golden heart and had hung it on a golden thread. He had requested that the heart be engraved with a prayer and a promise: *Pinky and Quizzle Forever.* Just to be clear, a *prayer* and a *promise* is different from a sacred *wish.* This *prayer* and this *promise* were Pinky's to give. Pinky's parents watched with concern, hoping his little heart would never be broken. Pinky's parents worried so! The kettle whistled a merry tune, and soon Pinky and his parents shared a lovely Christmas Eve dinner with all the trimmings.

When it was time for bed, Pinky put on his pyjamas and stood by the window. With his paw in his pocket still holding his sacred wish, he gazed out at the night sky, trying to imagine where Quizzle might be. He had been missing her all day! He felt a pang squeeze hard in his heart. A tear rolled down his lovely but lonely little face. Without intending to make a wish, he squeezed the stone in his pocket, and he squeezed it hard! He just needed something to hold on to.

"I wish...I wish I had wings!" he said. "Then I could fly, too." Now this was a wish from the heart! Pinky could feel a tug on his back, and he reached 'round to give it a scratch. "Oh my," he whistled.

Pinky had wings!

Pinky's whole furry body vibrated with glee! The light in his room cast shadows of his wings on the wall. Pinky's new wings were not of the feathery kind. Nor were they translucent like Quizzle's or Dragonfly's wings. Pinky had furry wings, as one may have guessed. Pinky's wings reflected his mood, and, in this moment, they shone with all the colours of the rainbow, every imaginable colour and hue. They shone with pure joy!

Now Pinky had never thought to use his wish for wings, but as soon as he did, he remembered his *Me*! At first, Pinky could hardly get control of his wings. In fact, the first place he flew was into a wall! He landed with a smack and fell flat, flat on his back! But the brave Pinky stood up and brushed himself off. He truly was a quick study, and soon he was soaring 'round his room with his eye on the moon. Then the brave Pinky Palm leapt out his window and soared up into the night sky.

What he had then was just like a bird's-eye view! Only it wasn't a bird's, it belonged especially to him. *Ah, ah!* he rejoiced, *I have a new Me! This is the Me I wanted to be!* He flew high above the tiny world he knew so well. He could see the whole village and all of the trees. He could see Redbush Ranch. He could see Quizzle's hive and the Garden of Everywhere. He could see creatures large and small. What's more than all this, Pinky could see endless possibilities in a world twinkling with dreams.

"Wow!" he whispered to himself. "Wow!"

Now, as many folks know, if you're going to take flight on Christmas Eve night, there is no end of traffic in the sky. Pinky had to watch where he was going! The sky was aflutter with all sorts of fairies and angels and such. Most of them were very small and difficult to see. A spark here and a twinkle there gave little notice they were in the air. If you were to gaze up from below, they might not even be seen. There was one who couldn't be missed, however. Climbing up through the sky, with a twinkle in his eye and his hand on the rein, was Santa Claus and his reindeer. With a big smile Pinky waved to Santa. Santa waved back.

"Ho! Ho! Hi Pinky!" Santa said.

Now this was a whole lot better than hiding behind a Christmas tree, down on the ground, just to watch Santa eat a cookie and drink some milk!

As Santa's laughter and his sleigh disappeared into the night, the sky became very quiet and ever so still. Pinky noticed the stillness and took in a deep breath. Somewhere between his breath in and his breath out, Pinky noticed the pure, sweet taste of love in his mouth and a tickle on his left ear.

"Merry Christmas, Pinky," Quizzle said, with a tender sigh. She had so hoped for this moment. Now Pinky could fly!

Pinky and Quizzle Forever! he thought.

Together they flew in perfect balance. They danced with the light well into the night. Pinky was so grateful for his new wings; he couldn't help but hum a little tune as he circled 'round the moon. Quizzle thought him most rare and couldn't help but twinkle and gaze at the magnificent Pinky. Then a slow, sliver of light gently touched the night. Dawn was near.

Quizzle, having had a very busy day and night, knew it was time to rest. Pinky flew her home, right to the door of her sweet little nest. Around her neck he tenderly placed the golden heart that said, 'Pinky and Quizzle Forever' and then...He *kissed her goodnight! Wow!*

On this Christmas night, all wishes came true! There wasn't a thing left to do but turn out the light. Now remember one is never alone. In the dark, there's always a spark. Goodnight!

Pinky had wings!

It's A Dog's Life

On one fine spring day, Mrs. Grupple basked in the sun and cooled off in the mud. She had no complaints; well, maybe just one. She was dreaming again of her dear friends in the forest. She hadn't been able to get into Tree Forest all winter and, my goodness, she had tried! The problem was that the password had changed. Mrs. Grupple didn't know that every year the password to get into Tree Forest changed from *raindrop* in summer to *snowflake* in winter. Mrs. Grupple was still using the summer password! Everyone, including Quizzle, had forgotten to tell her this important fact. Mrs. Grupple had just about given up, but *just about*, you see, just wasn't enough. She couldn't stop recalling her twinkly, colourful friends and wondering where they might be.

What she didn't know was that her friends were thinking of her, too, wondering why she hadn't come to visit them all winter! In fact, they hadn't seen her since they had all saved Quizzle and her angel, Titania, from Wag, the wicked witch. That was last Halloween!

So, Mayor Justintime and Mrs. Grupple's friends called a town meeting to set up an official search for the pooch. Mayor Justintime and her Gingerbread Council sent out very formal municipal notices to anyone who might have had official business with the pooch. She also sent a short just-in-case note to the animal rescue foundation and a query to Redbush Ranch.

In the meantime, Skunk was elected to lead the expedition. With one's nose following Skunk, it was hard to get lost.

Mr. Quiggle, a little-known *snake in the grass*, had a printing press and made up all sorts of flyers that read: DOG WANTED, to post on some very accommodating trees. Pinky, who was very good at drawing, drew maps, and Quizzle sparked everyone's interest. They all wanted to help find Mrs. Grupple.

What they didn't know was that Mrs. Grupple wasn't lost, and she didn't need rescuing. She just wanted to be reunited with her friends. She had been *shut out* of Tree Forest! The trees in Guardian Grove took their jobs very seriously; some might venture to say too seriously.

Mrs. Grupple had done everything she knew how to do. She'd looked into the grove with her most baleful, brown-eyed stare. This had always worked on her two-legged mistress, but not on these trees! Then she'd tried to nose her way in, but a prickly bush soon put a stop to this tactic. One day, when her nose was better, she stood up on her two hind paws and out-and-out begged, with whimpers and moans. The fortress was tight, and the trees tried to explain, "Rules are rules for a reason."

To Grupple, this just didn't make sense. One morning, out of sheer frustration, she peed on a tree, but the tree wouldn't budge. In response, the whole of Guardian Grove just shook and soaked her with dew. By this time, Mrs. Grupple was beginning to feel outnumbered. She picked herself up, shook herself off, and made up her mind not to try again—until tomorrow, that is.

The next day, Grupple finished her daily roll in the dirt and headed out once again for Tree Forest to find her dear friends. Grupple wasn't the scheming sort—she liked to play it by ear. She had no plan, just a big heart filled with desire as she made her way back to the woods. She sniffed all about, putting her faith in her snout. The air was sweet with spring flowers and dung as Grupple hung out her tongue. Her tail wagged with glee when she spied a bee flying by, but the bee was busy and couldn't stop to play. Grupple understood and carried on with her quest. Along the way, she sniffed a gnome right out of his home. The gnome shook his fist and told Grupple to *get lost*. Not a very happy gnome! Mrs. Grupple obeyed, but she didn't get lost, just out of the way.

It wasn't long before Grupple found herself yet again at the edge of the woods. The trees in Guardian Grove noticed this and sunk their roots deeper into the earth. A little wildflower called out to a fern, "Here she comes again!"

This time, Grupple tried to reason with the lot. "I've been here before," she explained. "The password worked once, so why not again?"

"None of your business!" piped up a birch. "Rules are rules."

"What then," asked Grupple in a reasonable tone, "if we changed the rule?"

"*Change a rule*! Did you hear that?" sputtered an outraged, gnarled, old Garry oak.

Grupple was beginning to alter her, thus far, good opinion of Guardian Grove. She started to dig a big hole. Dirt went flying everywhere as she dug with a fury. Grupple still didn't have a plan; she just started to dig because she was upset. But her hole was getting very deep. As she was digging, her paw hit a root, the root of a tree.

"Ouch," said the tree. "Get away from me!"

Now dear Mrs. Grupple didn't want to hurt anything or anyone—not even a flea, as one may recall. "So sorry!" she said to the sensitive tree. The tree cried a torrent and then sniffed himself 'round to accepting Mrs. Grupple's most humble and sincere apology as she put back his ground.

When the remorseful Mrs. Grupple had just about filled the hole back up, a thoughtful young fern raised an inquisitive frond to one of her elders—a fifty-ring tree. She had a question to ask, though it took her great courage to query an elder. She had been inspired by Mrs. Grupple's example to never give up. "What if..." the fern queried, "what if this pooch is telling the truth? What then?"

At this, the fifty-ring tree felt an ancient *chill-breeze* ruffle his leaves.

"Hmm?" said the tree, and then he peered way down at Grupple and said, "As you may know, my dear dog, Guardian Grove has a very important job to do, to keep one and all safe. How can we know it is the truth that you speak?"

The tree cried a torrent and then sniffed himself 'round...

"Hmm," said Mrs. Grupple as she shook out her head. "I guess I could leave you some sort of a guarantee, perhaps a tasty bone or some I.D. But the thing is, I have nothing on me. Perhaps you would be willing to take my word instead?"

"Take your word?" said the fifty-ring tree. "What you want is our trust?"

The elder tree gazed around at the whole of Guardian Grove. He noticed his gaze was met with some encouraging glances. He looked back over at the hopeful young fern who had raised the question. *Hmm*, thought the elder, *we really must show a measure of trust*. The fifty-ring tree gazed at Grupple for a good long time, hemming about this and hawing about that. Grupple met his inquisitive eye with not even a blink. Then the elder tree cleared his throat. He seemed as though he had arrived at some sort of decision. "Oh, do come right in," he said with a warm chuckle.

Mrs. Grupple wasn't going to miss this opportunity, but not before a big thank you bark and a wag of her tail at the kindly elder and the sweet young fern.

"This is a trust I will never forget," she said as she dashed right on in.

The forest was so pretty this time of year, and Mrs. Grupple didn't forget to stop and smell a wild little flower as she made her way in. The wildflower said nothing for once. Mrs. Grupple traveled, nose to the ground and tail in the air, up her old path. She remembered her first visit here for Quizzle's flying up party, but that was a long time ago and so much had happened since then.

Grupple came to a bridge and had begun to cross when she heard a muffled sound as if it were coming from under somewhere. She stopped to listen, surprised by what she'd heard. From under the bridge came a "*Boo*!" and a "*Hoo*!"

Mrs. Grupple looked over the rail. "What's wrong?" she whispered to someone she could not see.

"Nothing, just go away," said a sad voice.

"Hope you're feeling better soon," mumbled a concerned Grupple as she went on her way.

Before long, Grupple came to a sign. The sign pointed and said, "Hello Mrs. Grupple. Justaroundthebend is that way."

"Oh, thank you, I know," answered Grupple politely as she followed her nose. Grupple was beginning to sense the town's smells. She could detect the bakery and a hot dog stand, too. She could most certainly estimate the location of the town barn. Grupple was so focused on her nose, though, that she had forgotten to look where she was going up close. She lost her footing, tripped on a rake, and rolled right into town. When she found her four paws and had dusted herself off, she noticed no one was home. Grupple sighed a deep sigh and looked around for a bone.

She walked past the bakery. The sign in the bakery door read: OUT TO LUNCH. She walked past the butcher, and the sign on the door read: GONE FOR LUNCH TOO.

"Lunch!" said Grupple, who was getting so hungry that she started to drool. "Then they should be back soon," she remarked. What Grupple didn't know was that the town was not *out to lunch.* The townsfolk just didn't have a sign that said what it was they were actually doing: SEARCHING FOR MRS. GRUPPLE. Their signs were too few.

Mrs. Grupple found a bone and settled down for a chew. When she finished her lunch, she meandered around and soon came across a sign in a window. This sign read: DOG WANTED.

That's me! she thought with a thrill, and she scratched at the door. No answer! Mrs. Grupple decided to give up on signs, but not on her friends. She waited and waited and waited some more. *Someone*, she thought, *is bound to come out of the store!*

Meanwhile, all the citizens of the whole town of Justaroundthebend searched for their four-legged friend (who, by the way, wasn't lost). There were dozens of folks and they marched down the path after Skunk. Well, some of them marched and some of them flew. Pinky and Quizzle noticed that progress was slow, but not everyone could fly, and this was an expedition for the whole town. Rock rolled along ever so slowly, and Mayor Justintime waddled from side to side. Millie Mole was getting so tired that Ricky Rabbit had to give her a piggyback ride. The fleas, who, as one may recall, had moved out in a snit, decided to join the expedition, too. They missed Mrs. Grupple, their old haunt. Their baggage was packed, and they were going to move back!

Finally, the fleas and all the searchers arrived at Guardian Grove.

The trees whispered as the villagers walked by. "Wait a moment," they said. "Mrs. Grupple went that way."

"Oh no!" squeaked Millie as they all scratched their heads.

"We can't go back now!" exclaimed Skunk "We're all so tired; let's have a nap in the barn." The whole town agreed. They trudged their way out of Tree Forest as Pinky and Quizzle flew ahead to fix up camp. The sun was just beginning to set in the west as the town of Justaroundthebend, dog-tired, entered Redbush Ranch.

One little barn swallow gazed down from her perch under an eave, just in time to see the whole scene. "A circus is coming! A circus is coming!" she tweeted, as the little town came around the bend.

The barn was in utter chaos, and this made no sense at all to the resident horse of Redbush Ranch. There were critters in the hay and fairies in the air, buzzing, jumping, and flying everywhere. They all seemed to know what they were doing, however, each intent on their own goal. Some carried water while others gathered food. Some made up beds while another stirred the pot. Quizzle flew around, lighting little fairy lanterns with her spark, and Pinky lent a paw, or a wing, to anyone who needed help with whatever it was they were doing. Looking at the big picture from outside to in, it might not make sense, although one couldn't but grin.

Back in Justaroundthebend, Mrs. Grupple looked up as the sun began its solemn descent, and she decided to start back for home, her head hanging low. She had lost interest in the trees and the bees and the flowers, she was so lonely. She barely looked up as she padded her way back, from the place she had come to the place she would go.

Just as the sun's glow was fading, Mrs. Grupple nosed her way back through Guardian Grove. This time the trees were asleep and didn't even notice Mrs. Grupple slump by, a tear in her eye. Arriving at Redbush Ranch, Mrs. Grupple snuffled her way through the yard and up the porch steps. Her two-legged mistress opened the door to her scratch and in she went for the night. *At least one door is open*, she thought. Mrs. Grupple lay by the fire and didn't even eat the food her mistress put out. One might say that she'd lost her play; she'd had such a frustrating day!

She wondered about her friends and where they might be.

Then along came a flea. "Oh, you're back," Grupple acknowledged with a scratch. The flea climbed all the way into Grupple's ear and whispered a big secret. Grupple listened to this tiny voice, and her ears perked right up. Grupple jumped away from her fire and out she went again.

The little barn swallow, which by this time had made friends with the lot, flew right into the barn with the news. "Mrs. Grupple is coming! Mrs. Grupple is coming!" Hummingbird hummed and Dragonfly flew. Mayor Justintime woke up from her nap just in time; Rock rolled about; Millie Mole gave a squeak, and Ricky Rabbit hopped the Hip Hop! The judge took just-a-peek to see what was going on. Titania, the dear little guardian angel, dipped her fingers into the treats, and Quizzle and Pinky soared right up to the rafters with glee. They all did what they do, one might say. Even the bee, who was busy before, arrived at the door.

When Mrs. Grupple nosed her way in, she was dazzled by the light and completely surprised and adored! The young ones swung from her coat and slid down her tail. The fleas moved back home, and Ricky Rabbit played a very merry tune on his fiddle while Quizzle, Pinky, Hummingbird, and Dragonfly all danced in the air. It was a grand affair!

Quizzle flew down to greet her dear friend. "Hi Mrs. Grupple. Good to see you again!" she whispered into her friend's floppy-down ear. Grupple's tail wagged in time with the tune, and she jumped and she played. She bound up and down from the ground to the air to the ground. What a happy hound!

Now, some would say, *It's a dog's life*, and perhaps, at the end of this particular day, it was true. Mrs. Grupple, for one, was having a ball! Goodnight from the whole sleepy town. See *ya* around.

TT's Trust

As the bright spring sun peeked her way into the woods, the fairies stretched their wings and shook off the dew from the previous night. The Garden of Everywhere glistened with light as the fairies picked up their morning assignments. Quizzle's parents gently tapped each fairy on the head with a wand and a whisper as each one climbed out of bed. Auntie Hoolahoop prepared them a meal of lemon drops and fairy food, such as *suptatumps* and *poons*. There were countless hives in this garden, and each hive held at least one or two fairies. Fairies lived for each moment and never grew weary. They just did what they do.

Fairies never knew from one day to the next what their assignments would be. Sometimes their assignments were only a twinkling inkling. Quizzle tried to decipher her clue. The task her father had whispered into her ear was simply this: "Teach TT to trust."

Quizzle wondered who 'TT' might be. Off she flew with her guardian angel on her shoulder. They didn't know where; they just flew through the air. They flew over the quarry and dipped their toes into a pond. They flew through some trees and around a bright web that shone in the sun. Quizzle and Titania tried to keep their eyes open for anything unusual and anyone in need.

It wasn't long before they ran into 'nake, a snake who had lost his S.

"Have you found your S yet?" Quizzle sang out as she fluttered above.

"Not yet, but I'm 'till looking," the determined little 'nake said.

"We'll keep an eye out, too," Quizzle replied. She wondered at first if 'nake was her assignment, but his name started with the currently lost S, not a *T*.

Quizzle put her wings into gear and flew here and flew there looking for clues. Titania was curious, too. They buzzed through a blink and a wink and some smiles, and still, they hadn't found what to do. Overhead flew a heron, all shiny and blue, and they waved to her as she slowly climbed higher into the air. She squawked out her call from a time before all, stretched out her long neck, and nodded her head as she glided away.

Soon they came upon two beavers as their tails hit the river, but all was okay with them. Then Quizzle and Titania soared up through some clouds bursting with rain. They got a bit damp but tried it again. Quizzle and Titania were having a very good time, but the morning was passing, and still, Quizzle hadn't found her assignment. "TT," she said to herself. "Teach TT to trust." And she knew she must.

Quizzle ran into a group of teddy bears having a picnic, and though surprised by their miniature guests, the bears invited Quizzle and her angel to join them. Quizzle politely declined, asking the bears if they knew anyone by the name of TT. The bears scratched their heads. "No one by that name," the big brown one said.

Pretty soon, they heard the call of a loon. Quizzle set herself down gently on one of the loon's fine feathers and asked, "Do you know who TT is?"

"*Who-hoo? Who-hoo?*" the loon asked, just to make sure she had heard the name right.

"TT," Quizzle said again.

"*No-oo, no-oo,*" the loon said with an echo in her voice.

Quizzle asked everywhere she flew, but no one seemed to know who TT was. She finally decided that she needed help from a friend to pick up the scent of this TT, and off she flew to see...guess who? She flew above Guardian Grove, and one of the tall trees called up to her, "Don't forget to stop by for a drop of dew next time you're in the neighbourhood!"

"I'll stop by very soon," Quizzle called back. She wanted to have a wee chat with those trees.

Quizzle landed on a branch at Redbush Ranch. Mrs. Grupple was so pleased, she leapt into the air and sniffed Quizzle's wing. Even the fleas were overjoyed, and they hopped up and down. "It's Quizzle! It's Quizzle! Hi Quizzle!" they cried. Quizzle made a motion, and they all settled down.

"I'm here on a secret mission," she said. Even the fleas perked up their ears as Quizzle explained about TT and her assignment of trust. Mrs. Grupple, who was only too happy to help, joined the search with her snout.

Following behind Grupple and her enthusiastic ride-a-long fleas, they all headed back for Tree Forest. The trees in Guardian Grove welcomed Quizzle and Mrs. Grupple, too! Mrs. Grupple sniffed and she sniffed, wondering what a TT smells like. She sniffed under a leaf and into a log that was just lying around.

Out popped the same old gnome, fist in the air.

"I thought I told you—" he started to say. Then he looked up and saw Quizzle hovering there. "Pardon me, Miss," he said with great reverence as he climbed right back in. It was good to have friends in high places.

As they arrived at a clearing in the woods, they looked up and could see a magnificent creature soaring through the skies. His wings were shiny and slick. When he saw them, he spiralled down through the blue with the grace of an eagle. As he drew near, Quizzle and her friends noticed this rather colourful *eagle* had a tail and a long furry one at that! Pinky swooped in and touched down for a three-point landing—tail and toes—right near his favourite friends.

"Hi Pinky!" they said.

"What's up?" he asked.

"We're looking for TT!" said the little angel.

Quizzle explained her mission of trust, and Pinky joined in as they carried on with their quest. Then they ran into Rock, who just rolled right in, joining the search for TT.

Soon they came to a bridge that they had all crossed before. From under the bridge came a "*Boo*!" and a "*Hoo*!"

Mrs. Grupple calmly explained, "He doesn't like to be bothered." One may remember Grupple had had a brief exchange with this one under the bridge during her last trip to town. She hung her head over once more, though, just to be sure. "Can we do anything for you? Anything at all?" she asked with great sympathy.

"I told you to leave me alone! Just go away!" sobbed the voice from under the bridge.

Quizzle looked at Grupple. The concerned Mrs. Grupple looked up with a furrowed brow. Pinky tested the strength of the bridge railing just in case. Rock, who thought he may have recognized the voice, rolled a little closer to the edge. They each wondered about who this sad one could be under the bridge. They decided further investigation was in order.

Rock rolled towards the bank. Grupple stretched herself over the edge to peer under, gripping the bridge with her hind paws. Pinky hung down from the bridge rail, with his tail, to get a better view. With Titania at her side, Quizzle flew tentatively in the direction of the voice that had called out. From upside down, Pinky thought he could see a shiver and quiver under the bridge.

TT looked up from his slumped posture, tears in his eyes. He'd been under this bridge for years, dealing with his wounded soul in the dark—not to mention a very bad headache. He certainly had no idea he had become anyone's special assignment! He had spoken with no one except to say, "Go away." And no one had spoken with him, except one, until today.

Suddenly, he was surrounded by friends, but he was yet to know this. TT looked up and saw two upside-down noses, attached to two upside-down heads, which were sniffing at him! Hovering in the air, he saw a glistening freckle-faced, red-headed fairy with a bejewelled angel at her side. *Perhaps I'm fading away?* he thought. TT was stunned. His mouth opened wide, but he couldn't make a sound. He was terrified!

The upside-down head with the rainbow-coloured tail said, "Hello," in a very soft voice, but TT couldn't talk back and just trembled instead.

Next, the creature with the yellow, upside-down snout and the upside-down brown eyes said, "Wanna play fetch?" At this TT heard a thump on the bridge!

"Oh no! He's come back!" TT screamed as he curled up even tighter.

The one thump, however, didn't belong to a *he* coming back. It belonged to an enthusiastic furry yellow *she*, as one may have guessed. It sounded nothing like a *tip-tap*, a *trappity-trap*, or even a *klumph*! It was just one soft *thump*, an invitation to play. But now Mrs. Grupple tucked her tail in.

Then the whole lot chanted, "Are you okay?"

After being frozen in fear and able to speak little more than a sputter, TT finally found his voice and shrieked out, "No! Go away! I don't want to play!"

At this, his *aspiring* new friends flew into a freaked-out furl and a whirl and suddenly disappeared from view. Now *they* were scared, too! TT's shriek was a blood-curdling sound! Taking just a moment, while it echoed around, Quizzle, Titania, Pinky, and Grupple were able to catch their breath.

"We can do this," Quizzle said.

"He's just scared," Pinky replied. "Perhaps he's lost his *Me*?"

They whispered encouragements to each other as they shook off their fear. Rock just waited.

Again, they put their heads together on the bridge.

"It seems that he scared us and we scared him," Pinky said.

"Perhaps we should leave?" wondered Grupple, wanting to be polite.

"I think we need to come up with a plan," Quizzle declared.

Rock stonily teetered on the edge. They all noticed Rock who was just about to fall over, and they rolled him right back. "Hmm... I have a faint memory of this voice," Rock said. Now Rock had been around since the beginning of time. Some memories do fade, but this one, it seemed, was trying to inch its way back. If Rock had a hand, he would have scratched his head.

"Perhaps we should send just one of us down," Quizzle suggested. They all agreed, but at first, no one quite knew who the *one* should be. Pinky was uncertain if TT was quite ready to meet an *everyanimal*. He looked at Quizzle. Quizzle scratched her head wondering if trolls are familiar with fairies, and Mrs. Grupple wagged her tail in anticipation.

Rock finally volunteered. "I could just roll down into the stream. I'm sure he's seen rocks before, and perhaps he needs a familiar face."

They all agreed, so Rock turned good-naturedly and rolled right back to the edge. This time, with a little push from his friends, over he went.

With a splash, Rock found himself right under the bridge, but still at some distance from the voice.

"Go away! Go away!" TT said.

"What's your name?" Rock patiently asked. He was surprised when his voice echoed so loudly under the bridge. "It's okay, I come as a friend." Rock's whisper was now soft and smooth, like butter on bread.

"I have no friends," TT sputtered. "Now you get out!"

"I will if you insist, but I do believe we met long ago. Perhaps if you could just whisper your name?" he gently probed. A long silence ensued. Rock was just getting ready to call for a roll back up when from deep in the dark under the bridge where no one could see, came the answer.

"I'm TT the Troll!."

Quizzle, hearing this from up on the bridge, realized TT the Troll was her assignment. She listened some more.

"My name's Rock, wouldn't you know?" Rock said with rare humor. "What does TT stand for?" he asked in a relaxed gentle way. Rock was very good with others, as he had an old soul.

"Too Tired to Trust," answered TT the Troll with an ancient sigh.

Rock furled his bumpy brow and said, "If you include yourself—" And then, after some mathematical calculation, finished with, "you're six T's short. Shouldn't it be TT, TT, TT, TT for TT The Troll Too Tired To Trust?"

"Just call me TT for short," said the Troll, feeling a little annoyed and confused. Trolls, as one may be aware, are not very good at arithmetic. In fact, TT could only count to three.

"Okay. TT for short," Rock said kindly.

While the others waited and listened quietly on the bridge, Rock carried on with his chat. "So, TT," Rock said. "You must have trusted a lot to have become so tired of it."

"I trusted three times, and that's three times too many! Promises,

promises!" bemoaned TT as new tears flowed. Now TT seemed to want to talk about his troubles.

"What happened?" Rock queried.

"*The three billy goats Gruff* happened, and they happened to me!" TT replied.

"What did these goats do to you?" Rock asked.

"They tricked me! I've been hungry ever since and I have a very sore head!" declared TT; and indeed, this was true.

"Oh yes it's all coming back to me now," Rock said. "In fact, one of the goats briefly stood on *me*."

"You *let* one stand on you!" TT howled. "How *could* you?"

"Oh, I was just there," Rock said. "But TT, my friend, do tell me what happened to upset you so much?"

"Well," TT said, "it was long past my lunchtime when I heard a little billy goat *tipping* and *tapping* over my bridge." TT paused.

"And then what happened?" Rock asked.

"Well, I explained to the little goat that he was about to be my lunch, but he didn't seem to like the idea."

"Hmm," Rock said, "I see. And then what happened?"

"Well, he made a promise to me. I can't remember the exact words but the drift of it was he had a bigger, juicer brother, well worth delaying my lunch for."

"Oh?" Rock said.

"I believed him!" bemoaned TT. "I believed every word that little goat said!"

"And then?" questioned Rock.

"Well, I agreed to wait for the bigger, juicer lunch of course. What troll in his right mind wouldn't choose a bigger lunch?" TT said with reminiscent bravado.

"And..." Rock said.

"I waited and I waited, and I was getting so hungry! But sure enough, along came a bigger brother."

"A—" Rock started to say, but TT quickly interrupted.

"I know what you're going to ask me now, Rock," TT continued. "Well, the bigger brother tricked me too. He promised the next brother would be a very, very big catch. What troll in his right mind wouldn't choose a super deluxe feast over a mid-sized banquet!"

"And so, that's what you did," Rock surmised.

"Oh, yes, that's what I did alright. And I waited!"

"Then what happened?" Rock asked although he was more than beginning to get the picture.

"Well," TT said. "That's the part I can't talk about."

"It's okay, no need," Rock patiently said. In fact, Rock knew what happened next because he was there. Rocks often go unnoticed. The third billy goat was a very big fellow. Very big indeed! He was enormous! He had no trouble bonking TT right on the head with his great, gigantic horns. TT had been under his bridge ever since, hiding his hunger and living with dread!

Anyone who has read the story *The Three Billy Goats Gruff* knows about the promises they made to the troll who lived under a bridge. Well, it appears that that troll was TT! Rock and his friends on the bridge listened while TT told the whole story, and Rock watched as TT's tears flowed into the stream. TT began to feel better for the attention and uncurled a little from his slump. A slump is when the body curls into a ball to keep the heart warm.

TT's heart was warming up a little. "I've been doing all the talking," said TT. "Tell me a little about you, Mr. Rock."

"Oh, don't call me *mister;* Rock is just fine." Then Rock thought a bit. "Well, I've been around for a very long time," he said. Then Rock asked, "Do you mind if I roll a little closer?"

"If you must," came TT's hesitant reply. Rock rolled just a little closer into the flow of the stream.

"You're getting quite deep," TT observed.

"Perhaps a little closer, then," Rock said, edging his way up. TT uncurled a little more and gazed down at Rock with his eyes opening wide.

"Watch out for my toes!" he said. TT looked cold and damp, and he was covered with slime. Indeed, it looked as though he had been under that bridge for a very long time.

Words echoed under the bridge as Rock and TT talked. "You look so cold," Rock said with care.

"Just stay over there," TT implored.

"I'm right here," Rock said. TT looked at Rock, and Rock gazed back. They each thought the other quite handsome but funny looking. Rock smiled a slow, sure smile, and TT smiled a little, too. Their smiles grew so large that they finally turned into outright laughs! TT and Rock laughed louder and louder. Their echoes now resounded from under the bridge. They laughed so hard their tummies hurt with the effort. "Mind if I turn on the lights?" Rock asked, and they both laughed some more.

Then Rock made his big move. "Come with me, TT," he said. By this time, TT had completely uncurled from his slump, and his heart was warmer than warm. TT thought for a moment and looked at Rock with a questioning eye.

"Maybe," TT said.

TT looked at Rock, and Rock looked at TT again. TT slowly climbed down from his ledge and dipped one toe in the water. Rock watched patiently while TT dipped yet another toe and then another until his whole foot was in.

"Good for you!" Rock said. TT looked up with a smile.

"Good for me!" TT repeated out loud.

TT didn't know it yet, but he had four more friends on the bridge. Ever so slowly but surely, Rock and TT came out from under the bridge and into the sun. TT the Troll was chubby and green, patched with blue. He had brown eyes and matte brown hair. To be honest, he looked a bit of a wreck and was in need of a bath, with soap to deal with the smell. TT had been in the dark for so long that his eyes had to squint. When his eyes had adjusted to the light, he couldn't believe what he saw! But with Rock by his side, he resisted a big urge to run and hide.

On the bridge were a curious lot, and now TT was curious, too. Rock introduced TT to each one. Grupple gave a tentative sniff. The guardian angel with the lavender hair danced along with some fleas on Mrs. Grupple's tail. Pinky soared in a congratulatory loop and Quizzle floated on a gentle breeze. They were all so pleased!

TT pulled himself up the bank, leaving a green, slimy trail. Mrs. Grupple's sensitive nose twitched at the odor. He really did stink! TT, who hadn't had company for so long, stammered a bit and stuck his toe in the ground. He was feeling quite shy.

"You must be ever so hungry," Mrs. Grupple supposed. "Let's have a picnic!" Mrs. Grupple loves food, but it was the wrong thing to say. TT was reminded of his earlier misfortune and the time he had been tricked out of his lunch. He started to cry.

"There, there," Quizzle said in an attempt to soothe the troll. "Would you keep your promise if *you* were the lunch?" TT's eyes opened wide. He thought about this. He thought about this hard, then after a moment pulled himself together, and lifted himself up.

"Oh well," he sniffled, "perhaps a picnic would just hit the spot."

Pinky and Quizzle laid out the picnic blanket, and Quizzle waved up some food with her wand. They had quite a spread! They had buns with cheese and peanut butter sandwiches, a basket of berries, and tarts with cream. They even had some tender grass shoots, one of Pinky's favorites. Quizzle, of course, enjoyed her fairy food. For this meal, she savoured a big bowl of *timp-tumps*, after she picked out the lumps.

TT looked around at the chow, and since it all looked so strange, he spoke up and said, "Got any goat?" TT half chuckled at himself.

Rock chuckled with him. Pinky tactfully said, "Oh, I'm sorry. They've all gone away."

After lunch, they gave TT a bath in the stream. They combed out his hair and shined him right up. TT was learning to trust in the kindness of friends, but not all in one day. TT had a lot to sort out. He was ready for bed. He waved goodbye to his new chums and crawled back under his bridge. He curled himself up, but not in a slump. He peeked out at the stars. He remembered the goats, this time with forgiveness in his heart, and he quietly wondered where they'd all gone.

TT pulled himself up the bank, leaving a green, slimy trail.

"I saw your S!"

'Nake the Snake

The grass moved a little bit here and a little bit there, as 'nake made his way. He was still looking for his S. 'Nake had lost his S in a bet he shouldn't have made with someone with whom he shouldn't have played. He was so sorry now. Without his S, 'nake couldn't slither, and he couldn't slide. He'd lost his shimmy and shake. All 'nake could do was bunch himself up and wait for his end to catch up with his beginning. Oh, it's true, he could roll from side to side, but this was not his usual ride. He just wasn't the same without his S, so he kept on looking and looking. He wriggled around all day, with no time to play, in search of his S.

'Nake lived in Tree Forest, where there were all sorts of snakes in the grass, and over time 'nake had learned that some snakes were friends and others were not. One lesson was particularly hard: there was one little rattler tattler who liked to make bets that he never lost. Unfortunately, 'nake, who was still very naïve, fell in with this rattler for a fast game of cards. Eventually, he had nothing left to bet, so the rattler tattler had taken off with his S. 'Nake had been looking for his S ever since. He'd heard a rumor that the rattler had split town and left the S lying around, but as of yet, no one had seen it.

'Nake continued on his search. He stretched his body out as far as he could, and then waited for his tail to catch up with his head. He did it again and again. Sometimes he rolled from side to side, but where was the fun of being a snake?

As 'nake was rounding a bend in the grass, he came across a log that seemed to have a big voice. The voice inside the log was complaining about unwanted guests, just as ’nake stuck in his head. Inside the log was the same old gnome, cleaning up his home.

“Hello Mr. Gnome,” ’nake said in greeting.

“Oh, do come right in!” the gnome said sarcastically.

“Have you seen my S?” ‘nake asked.

“Your what?”

“My S. I lost my S in a bet,” explained ’nake.

“Then that’s what you get for gambling!” scolded the gnome from his pompous point of view inside his log. ’Nake wondered why this gnome was so grumpy; he had such a nice home.

“Sadly, I can’t stay for long,” ’nake said humbly as he pulled his head out of the log and went on his way.

’Nake next came to a meadow filled with spring flowers. The air was sweet, and busy with bees flying from one flower to another. ‘Nake stopped to look and saw one little bee who’d become stuck in a tulip. ‘Nake stuck out his tongue and flicked the bee free. “Thank you so much!” said the little bee, who buzzed herself off.

“No problem,” ’nake said as he moved on.

Eventually ’nake rolled over onto his back and looked up at the sky. There was his friend, Pinky. Pinky was soaring so free in the air. There was a sparkle-and-glint at his side; it appeared Quizzle, too, was along for the ride. Pinky performed a dive and a roll, and then glided right in. Quizzle hovered nearby on a gentle breeze.

“What are you looking for?” Pinky whistled to ‘nake.

“I lost my S,” ‘nake said.

“Oh my! Your S is still missing? This is serious,” Quizzle declared.

“Thank you; it is,” agreed ’nake, adding, “I haven’t felt the same ever *thinth*.” ‘Nake wiggled around with discomfort like he’d lost his best friend, and in a way he had. ’Nake begins with an S. Without his beginning, it was hard to fathom his end.

Pinky squinted at ’nake; to him, it was very clear something was missing, and it started with an S.

“Well let’s have a look,” whistled Pinky. And just like that, ’nake had two friends to share in his search.

Quizzle hovered here and flew over there. She examined every twist and every turn; she explored each curl and every swish and swerve. She looked at everything she could spy with her eye that came close to the shape of an S. At one point she felt sure she'd found it! But when she flew down, it turned out she'd only picked up the tail of a cat. Not much she could do about that. She put it right back and apologised sincerely to the ringtail cat.

The confused cat said, "No worries, eh," and scurried along.

Pinky searched from the air, and 'nake wiggled along on the ground. They looked all morning without any luck until they ran into a *muchaluck* named Tuck who'd heard tell of an S, somewhere around.

A muchaluck is a strange sort of creature and rarely seen. Muchalucks turn up when someone is down on their luck, as one might have guessed. They come in all sorts of colours, and this particular one was yellow and blue. Muchalucks come in all shapes and sizes, too. His body was mushy, like chewed gum, and he had short little legs. He hopped over to 'nake and gave him a break.

"I saw your S!" he declared in midair, before landing on 'nake's nose and gazing into his eyes.

'Nake's eyes opened wide.

"Where is my S?" he asked with surprise.

"You passed it a little way back," the muchaluck Tuck said.

'Nake wiggled around in good faith. He headed a little way back, and just guess what he found? He found an S—but it wasn't his S that he found stuck in the ground. This S belonged to someone else, and it didn't quite fit. 'Nake tried

it on anyway and thought he'd make do. Pinky and Quizzle soaring overhead could see 'nake slide around with his new large S, which was better than none at all for the time being.

Oh well, he thought, *I'll get used to this* S. But he didn't. It just didn't feel right. It wasn't *his* S.

From up in the sky, Quizzle thought she spotted something down on the ground. With the tip of her translucent wing, she pointed out this distant dark shape. Pinky soared in a little closer, and there, tucked into a ledge on a very high cliff, he could see a strange, mean-looking sort; it was a rattler tattler, of course. This rattlesnake was laughing out loud, his head in a cloud of his own bad breath. He had been playing solitaire, and he'd just beaten himself. He never could lose; however, he was a poor winner, too. Lying beside him, tucked into his bedroll, was a sad, lonely S. 'Nake's S missed him, too.

"I miss my 'nake!" the little S cried. "I miss my 'nake, and I want my 'nake!" it hollered. This little voice echoed through the mountains like a song—a song and a dance. "Where is my 'nake? I want my 'nake now!" the voice called.

The rattler was irritated by the little S that had interrupted his game, so he threw the S out. He tossed him right off of the cliff and said, "Don't come back!" Then he gave his tail a shake, and the sound it made sent a menacing scare into the air. His best game really *was* solitaire.

The S fell far but never had a chance to land; for, in no time, Pinky and Quizzle had him in hand. They soared through the sky, and the little S had a very good time enjoying the view. Soon they spotted 'nake, and down they flew. Pinky and Quizzle helped 'nake on with his very own S. They were a perfect fit. 'Nake was Snake once again!

Snake wiggled around in glee. It was a joy to see. Quizzle and Pinky had given him what seemed like a new beginning, and now he could fathom his end.

Mr. Grumpkin Goes for a Ride

Mr. Grumpkin, the gnome, peeked past his pink curtains and into the woods. He noticed some critters and creatures playing and laughing out loud. He grumbled some words about the loudness of noise and marched right out his door, fist in the air. "Be quiet, *you*!" he hollered.

Mr. Grumpkin lived in a lovely, large log home, outfitted with a big old-fashioned wood stove and a long dining table where he and his family had shared all their meals, and some tall tales too! There was a grand, gnome-sized, four-poster bed in the room he and his dear wife, Ethel, had shared. Compared to others, Mr. Grumpkin had done really quite well, especially with Ethel, who tended to even him out.

For the past few years, however, Mr. Grumpkin had been all alone. He'd been dragging his log home around from place to place looking for peace and quiet, which he still hadn't found. Sometimes he lived here, and sometimes he lived there, but no matter where he plunked his home down, there were others around, and *they all made noise*!

Mr. Grumpkin hated company, and he didn't like noise. Nor was he partial to games or toys. Mr. Grumpkin's first name was Fred; a name very few knew, for he preferred to be called *Mister*. He was a very formal sort of fellow and rarely on a first-name basis with anyone. Well, there had been one, and her name was Ethel, Mrs. Ethel Grumpkin. To Fred, she had been wed. Mr. Grumpkin was Fred to Ethel, and Ethel was Ethel to Fred, and to everyone else, too. Ethel wasn't the formal sort. The Grumpkins had had many children in their day, but they'd all moved away. Now that Ethel was no longer near, Mr. Grumpkin stayed at home, all alone.

Mr. Grumpkin's home was ship-shape, not a crumb on the floor nor a twig by the door. He cleaned up the dust before it ever touched down, and this kept him very busy all the day 'round. In fact, he kept up the fight much of the night. No dust, no mould, no spills or splats, no ticks or chips, no this and definitely no that. Mr. Grumpkin couldn't stop cleaning!

Knock, knock, knock came a sound at the door. Mr. Grumpkin carefully rinsed out his rag and stood his mop in its proper corner, grumbling to himself all the while. He went to the door and called out with great irritation, "Who's there?"

"It's me," came the answer. "It's me, Millie Mole."

"Millie who?" snapped the gnome.

"Millie Mole," Millie repeated nervously. Millie had summoned up all her courage to arrive at this place. Mr. Grumpkin opened his door and stuck out his nose, one eye, and half of his chin. In between there somewhere, was his mouth.

"What do you want?" he demanded.

"I'm baking cookies, and I've run out of milk," Millie answered.

"Milk!" exclaimed Mr. Grumpkin, "No, go away!"

Millie's whole little body started to shake as she stood at the door. She had never been spoken to in this fashion before. She turned on her heel and scurried away as fast as she could, followed by an echoing *slam, slam, slam.*

Perhaps Mr. Grumpkin had forgotten how much he had loved Ethel's freshly baked cookies.

Mr. Grumpkin went back to his cleaning with a plop and a plunk in his pail. He scrubbed his whole house cleaner than clean, thinking how pleased his dear Ethel would be if she could see it, and then he put some soup in a pot. As Mr. Grumpkin was preparing his lunch, he heard a big bang that shook him right up. He marched out his door and let out a roar. "*Stop that banging now!*"

Mr. Grumpkin opened his door and stuck out his nose, one eye, and half of his chin.

But by this time the one bang had stopped. He looked everywhere outside, but no one was there, so inside he went.

Mr. Grumpkin's soup was aboil. He set out his table with meticulous care and served himself up. All was blissfully quiet but for the noise he made as he sipped and he slurped and he sipped and he slurped... Mr. Grumpkin finished his lunch and dabbed at his chin with some satisfaction.

Just as he began clearing away his bowl, it started to pour. Rain poured down on Mr. Grumpkin's roof. The wind roared around his yard and under his door.

The rain went plip, plop, plip, plop, plop, plip. Every drop echoed in Mr. Grumpkin's big ears, which he soon covered up with some muffs. All was quiet now, at least for Mr. Grumpkin.

Then came the thunder he couldn't shut out!

"*Stop that noise*!" he screamed at the sky as he leapt out his door. Just then a thick, black cloud was passing by. The cloud shook his fist right back and followed Mr. Grumpkin as he ran here and as he ran there. Eventually, Mr. Grumpkin, all wet and covered with mud, found his way back into his house. Now there was mud on his floor!

Just as soon as Mr. Grumpkin had dried himself off and began to mop his floor again, another visitor arrived. It was Ricky Rabbit, and he was very cross with Mr. Grumpkin. In fact, he was spoiling for a fight. Ricky Rabbit had heard talk about the way Mr. Grumpkin had spoken to his dear Millie Mole, and he was here to lay down the law. Ricky thumped on the ground, and with all the ferociousness he could command, he called Mr. Grumpkin out into his yard. Now, Ricky Rabbit was a whole lot bigger than the gnome-sized Mr. Grumpkin, so Grumpkin locked himself tightly into his home instead.

Ricky Rabbit thumped a loud thump on Grumpkin's yard and left with a warning. "You will never be disrespectful to Millie again, or *else*!"

Or else what? wondered Grumpkin, who made not a sound. Mr. Grumpkin was not thinking of Ethel or how he would have defended her if she had been disrespected. Mr. Grumpkin was not having a very good day, and the rain continued to pour.

A short time later, Snake poked his head into the log house. He wanted to let Mr. Grumpkin know he'd found his S. Mr. Grumpkin stared an incredulous stare as if to say, *And you think I care?*

It wasn't long before TT stopped by to ask for some directions so he could visit his new friends. He was all squeaky and clean and well on his way. Mr. Grumpkin just said, "Why don't you just crawl right back under your bridge? Now get lost!"

TT left with a "*Boo*!" and a "*Hoo*!"

The rain poured so hard and for so long that Mr. Grumpkin's log started to slide. Grumpkin was going for a ride!

Fred Grumpkin peeked out from behind the pink, flowery curtains that his Ethel had sewn. He was surprised and more than a bit disgruntled to notice that his yard was moving! Or at least, to Grumpkin, it seemed as though his yard was moving.

"Stay where you are!" he demanded, but his yard continued to slip away. Mr. Grumpkin's house was gaining speed, and it seemed as if the whole world was passing him by. Mud seeped in under his door as his log slid down the bank of a stream and into the swift current, yet still, he stayed home. Grumpkin held on for dear life as his log rocked and rolled and twisted and turned through eddies and rapids. At once he was up, and then he was down. He was spinning around and around and around.

Mr. Grumpkin wasn't the only one trying to hold on. Along the way, he heard a tiny splash and a great big shout! It was Millie Mole and Ricky Rabbit trying to grab on. Mr. Grumpkin reached out and gave them a lift with a long nimble stick. Along the way, he noticed all sorts of creatures caught up in the storm and invited them on board. It seemed in this moment he really did care.

"Do come right in!" he said most sincerely, as they scrambled on board flipping and flopping all over his living room floor.

Then he noticed TT clinging to a soaking wet rock and gasping for air. This was not the Rock some have come to know, but nevertheless, TT was grateful for the assistance. Mr. Grumpkin threw him a rope, and TT held on. Mr. Grumpkin pulled and he pulled until finally, TT was within reach. This took no small effort if you think about the difference in size between a gnome and a troll. TT was many times Mr. Grumpkin's size!

But now that he was near, how on Earth would Grumpkin rescue TT? He just wouldn't fit in! On the other hand, he couldn't let him go. For TT this would be his certain demise.

Mr. Grumpkin looked deeply into TT's big brown eyes, which were brimming with tears. Normally, when Mr. Grumpkin ran into a puzzle, he would scratch his chin to help himself think; not an option here! Mr. Grumpkin needed both hands to keep TT afloat, and his beautiful log home was certainly no boat! Just as it appeared there was no solution in sight, TT was able to scramble up onto Grumpkin's front porch. With his ten toes curled onto Mr. Grumpkin's porch, he wrapped his arms around Mr. Grumpkin's log home and poked his green and brown, soaking wet head into Mr. Grumpkin's skylight window. What a sight he did see! Grumpkin had a full house!

"What are we going to do?" someone cried out in dismay.

Ricky Rabbit peeked out and noticed the stream had become a river, and the river was high. They were rounding a bend, and they all thought they could die.

But suddenly they stopped with a lurch and a jerk. At first no one wanted to move, including TT, lest the log not be secure. They stayed very still and decided the littlest one should creep to the window and check the scene out. Millie tied a long string to Ricky Rabbit's belt and then around her waist. She tipped and she toed her way to the window.

"Oh my!" she whispered as she nervously peered out.

"Where are we?" whispered several of the others as they clung to their spots.

"Well," Millie said as she searched for some words, "we are here. We have arrived."

Mr. Grumpkin and his guests teetered on the edge. But on the edge of what, they did not know.

Millie explained to the group, "We must have fallen up! All I can see is the sky below."

Hmm, thought the lot. No one wanted to move. Where would they go with the sky below? Mr. Fred Grumpkin and his crew stayed very still and very quiet. They listened for the sounds of what they could not see. From inside the soaking log, they listened carefully, and they listened long.

At first, they noticed what they didn't hear. They couldn't hear a plip or a plop. The rain had stopped. There was no thunder, no lightning, and no wind in the trees; not the call of a bird or the buzz of a bee. There were no barks or squeaks or squawks; no bells jingling, no creak of a gate on a hinge. No footsteps above or below. No one laughed, and certainly, no one played. They heard nothing, nothing at all.

Millie looked at Ricky, and Ricky looked at Mr. Grumpkin. From Mr. Grumpkin's skylight, TT peered down at them all. Also on board were some squirrels, some sweet little pocket mice, and a chipmunk or two. Their eyes opened wide. Mr. Grumpkin looked around at his house full of soaking wet guests. He felt grateful that, at least for now, they were all okay.

Then, suddenly, out of nowhere, came a knock at the door!

"Hello," Mr. Grumpkin said ever so softly as they all turned their heads.

"Who's in there?" questioned a soft, little voice.

"We all are," came the hopeful reply from Grumpkin.

"Everyone?" questioned the voice.

"The whole crew," Grumpkin answered.

"What are you doing?" the curious voice asked.

"Listening," TT said.

"Yes, but listening to what?" continued the voice.

"We're listening to you!" Ricky Rabit cried with relief.

"Oh, that's nice," the voice said tenderly. A single eye peeked into the log. "You've come right to the edge; would you like to go back?"

queried the voice.

"Oh... yes... please!" were their cries.

"Hold on then," the voice commanded, and hold on they did. Suddenly they were swooped up and gently placed down, down on the solid ground.

Ever so carefully, each one of the creatures in the house let go. Mr. Grumpkin brushed himself off. Ricky untied Millie's string from his belt. TT took a deep breath and ran his hands through his hair. The slightly confused chipmunks scratched their heads, and the dear little pocket mice sniffed at the air. It was time to step out!

Mr. Grumpkin opened the door and peeked around. The sun had come out, and the blue sky was bluer than blue. A warm, gentle breeze whispered, "Hello" to Mr. Grumpkin, who stood with his feet on the ground. One by one, each traveler stepped out, and they gathered together. They looked about to see who had saved them. They saw no one at all! Someone had been and someone had gone, or so it seemed.

They stood together, as if in a dream. Mr. Grumpkin's log home had been carefully placed exactly where it had been before the storm had washed it away. There wasn't a twig out of place, but something had changed, and Mr. Grumpkin realized it was him.

Mr. Grumpkin wasn't grumpy! After surviving all of this strife, he had a new lease on life! He had been so lonely and so sad for such a long time; he had lost his kind loving ways. Now he realized he'd been a selfish old ... goof. He looked around with great care and smiled softly at his bedraggled crew. Then he invited them to stay for some stew. He even poured a cup of milk for Millie. When he handed Millie the brimming cup, he looked at her with some sorrow in his eyes and said, "Can you forgive me, Miss?"

Millie knew what Grumpkin meant and nodded her head, smiling gently. She would bake cookies for dessert! The whole group thanked Mr. Grumpkin for saving their lives. Mr. Grumpkin looked at them shyly and said, "Oh, do call me Fred!"

From the highest branch of the tallest tree in Mr. Grumpkin's yard came the tiniest sparkle of a wing and a happy giggle.

One may never know when a fairy has come or gone. Sometimes we can only tell by reviewing the events of the day. Mr. Grumpkin and his newfound friends knew in their hearts that their troubles had been solved in a magical way. Have you had a visit from a fairy today?

Two for Dew

The bright yellow sun reached out her ribbons of warmth and light. Summer was a favorite time for the folks in Justaroundthebend and the surrounding forest. Quizzle and Pinky were down at the pond, cooling off in the water with a couple of otters. More folks ought to know that fairies can swim. Well, in fact, they swim very well! Quizzle loved to get her wings wet, and her wings loved it, too. She could use them like fins and swim very quickly; so quickly that at times, she was hard to spot.

The water sparkled in the sunlight, and one of those sparkles was Quizzle. It was difficult to tell just which one. By scrunching up one's eyes, and gazing without looking too hard at any one thing, a fairy might be spotted, and other times, not. Quizzle could stay underwater for a very long time, as she had learned to bubble-breathe. With her magic powers, she could make herself so tiny that she could slip right into a bubble and stay in there for as long as she liked.

Pinky loved to swim too, and sometimes when he was soaking wet, his homebody looked like an otter, only smaller. Pinky liked to swim very quickly underwater and then shoot himself up into the sky and fly. Now Pinky was flying around trying to spot the sparkle of Quizzle, but she was sitting on a lily pad, talking with a frog whom she'd never met before. The frog was telling Quizzle all about his travels to here and there and back again. She listened politely to the places this frog had been and then bid him adieu. Pinky and Quizzle had a lot to do on this bright summer's day. They were going to Guardian Grove to visit the trees. Ever since her flying up party, Quizzle had been promising those trees she'd stop by. Today was the day!

Quizzle and Pinky dried off in the sun and waved goodbye to Oggy and Ola, their two otter friends. Then they were off to Guardian Grove to sip some dew. The trees appreciated visits from friends, as they couldn't leave their roots. Pinky and Quizzle flew through the blue sky, enjoying a warm little breeze. The breeze began to tease them and eventually gave them a lift. Pinky and Quizzle did somersaults right there in the air, and then with a curl and a swirl, off the breeze laughingly blew.

Quizzle and Pinky giggled their way over the treetops as they played in the blue. They arrived in Guardian Grove just in time for dew. The trees were expecting them, too, and welcomed them in. The forest was cool and scented with spruce and pine. Some little wildflowers chimed out, "You're just in time!" Their petals shook in the breeze from Pinky and Quizzle's landing. Now Pinky and Quizzle were down on the ground.

The beautiful trees nodded their tops. "So glad you could come," welcomed a fir.

"Come sit on my branch," offered a kindly arbutus.

"Don't mind if we do," Pinky and Quizzle said in unison as they settled onto a branch already occupied by a sweet little red robin tucked into her nest. She was waiting patiently for her eggs to hatch. She was expecting four hatchlings, and she let Pinky and Quizzle have a quick peek.

A beautiful orange and black monarch butterfly landed there, too. She'd had a long flight all the way from the south and was a little weary.

She spoke with a cool, southern drawl.

"Hi y'all," she sighed.

"Hello, did you have a good trip?" Quizzle asked with interest as she sipped her dew.

"Why," she said in a breathy voice, "we had a lovely winter at our home in the south, but it's good to be back in the grove."

The forest was busy with all sorts of creatures flying and walking and crawling around. There were twitters and tweets and mushrooms and owls. There were ladybugs and gentlemen bugs, too. A whole army of ants marched up and proudly saluted the guests. Peeking out from the nooks and the crannies was a horde of inquisitive gnomes; they were a bit shy, though. The wildflowers danced in a rough little breeze, their petals all askew.

The trees, of course, stayed rooted in place. Quizzle wondered if they ever got bored with so little to do. As if in answer to her query, one little pine peeked all around, wiggled her roots out of the soil, and quietly tiptoed away. "Umm," worried Quizzle, and Pinky had noticed, too. The little pine didn't get far, however, before she was called back by her mother tree and re-rooted in her place.

Pinky wondered what it would be like to stay in one spot. He asked a giant oak with his thousandth-year ring what it was like being a tree. The oak smiled a slow, sure smile and calmly explained, "You just let the world come around you."

"Oh," said Pinky. *That must be a difficult task*, thought Quizzle. They each tried to imagine themselves still. The oak, however, looked quite content and pleased.

Suddenly, a little bell rang out through the woods, and all the gnomes climbed out of their homes. They all looked like they were going somewhere. "Where are you headed?" Pinky asked one.

A kindly old gnome looked up and explained, "We're off to pick berries from bushes and grapes from vines." Gnomes loved berries and grapes! These gnomes were quite small in stature and they preferred to blend in. They were all dressed in forest colours—green, red, and brown. Unlike dwarves, who whistle while they work, these little gnomes walked and chattered, all talking at the same time. They each seemed to understand, however, just what the others had said. It wasn't long before the noisy little crew disappeared from view.

Once again, the forest was still. Pinky and Quizzle sipped some more dew. It was charming in the grove; Pinky and Quizzle were very relaxed and very sleepy. They soon nodded off for an afternoon nap. They could hear a song in the trees, but it didn't have words. This song was a whisper, the whisper of leaves. Anyone who has lain face up on the ground and looked up through the trees will remember the streaming fingers of light that flow down. As Quizzle and Pinky slept, these fingers of light reached out and touched them; in fact, they picked them right up. Pinky and Quizzle were lifted gently to float in a world of dreams. Only their shadows were left on the ground.

Pinky's shadow stood up and stretched itself out. Quizzle's shadow danced around in the trees. Wee! Their shadows were free! Shadows have a hard job. They follow their host body around wherever they go, no matter how fast and no matter how slow. Well, actually, they do have a life of their own, but hardly anyone notices. Pinky and Quizzle's two shadows took this opportunity to let themselves loose and go their own way. It was time for the shadows to play!

Quizzle's shadow slid up a tree, with Pinky's shadow close behind.

They leapt from branch to branch and from pine to pine. The trees were accustomed to shadows and thought this quite fun. These little shadows were on the run. They ran through some leaves and leapt over a bush. They slid themselves along the ground, wiggling and scratching their backs like two dogs with an itch. Then they rolled around in a ditch.

Now, shadows are not polite guests. They are really quite different from the bodies we know. Pinky and Quizzle's shadows leapt up in the air and said, "Boo!" to the little red robin as she guarded her nest. Her feathers were a little ruffled, but she twittered politely to the guests.

"Boo!" they said to a passing gnome who stepped out of the way.

"Boo!" they said to a red-tailed squirrel as she clung to her branch.

These shadows were beginning to stir up some trouble. The thousand-year oak noticed this upheaval and bade them settle down on the ground. Pinky's shadow laughed right out loud in the old oak's face, while Quizzle's shadow just scratched her head and fluttered her dark wings with a devious smile. These shadows were not like Pinky and Quizzle at all! The shadow of Pinky gobbled up the contents of a barrel of dew, and the shadow of Quizzle grabbed some grapes from a gnome coming home. They took without asking and did just whatever they wanted to do! The trees and the creatures and critters in Tree Forest were growing concerned and called a meeting to discuss what they were going to do with their guests' rude little shadows.

The gnarly old Garry oak declared, "We'll send them right home!"

The gentle fern suggested they just wait a bit.

The weeping willow shed a tear.

All the gnomes arrived home, their baskets brimming with berries and grapes. The trees and some of the critters explained the situation to the gnomes, who then also had a group chat. One gnome suggested that they catch these two and tie them down until Pinky and Quizzle woke up. Another suggested they call in the *shadow catchers* from Justaroundthebend. A shadow catcher is somewhat like a dogcatcher, only they catch shadows instead.

Now the naughty little shadows were hanging upside down and shooting grapes at those on the ground. With a hiss and a snigger, they swung from a tree. Pinky's shadow asked, "How many points for a gnome?" as he aimed a big grape right at one's head.

"Stop that now or else!" demanded a pine. Quizzle's shadow laughed a discourteous laugh and spun herself into a dark little swirl.

"Oh my! Oh my!" worried the willow. Something had to be done about this rude kind of fun.

Pinky and Quizzle slumbered as they floated in the soft light of their sweet dreams, unaware of what was happening on the ground. Wrapped safely in a white, feathery cloud, they dreamt of sweetness and light. They entered a world filled with love and no fear. They danced together in a single dream as they sang to the moon and twinkled with stars—stars in their eyes, that is. In this dream, there was no place they couldn't go and not a thing they couldn't do. These were a powerful, limitless two.

Down on the ground, however, trouble did brew as the shadows flew. Pinky and Quizzle's shadows were so sick of goodness, sweetness, and light that they just wanted to fight! The shadow catchers had been summoned, and the whole of Guardian Grove was in an uncharacteristic improper mess. The gnomes had locked themselves tightly into their homes. The birds had flown, except one, who sat quivering alone on her dear little nest. The trees had taken a very firm stand. There was nothing they could do now but await the shadow catchers.

The shadows of Pinky and Quizzle eventually sat down for a rest. The trees tried to reason with them, but they weren't listening to a word the trees said.

A little wildflower piped up and declared, "You'd better watch out! The shadow catchers are coming for you!"

The shadows thought this was delightful and prepared for a game of hide and seek. "They'll never catch us!" they hollered as they tried to blend in. Shadows are very good at blending in. They hide in the dark and can do this even by day. When it's bright, shadows simply find larger shadows to hide in. These two hid in the long broad shadow of the thousand-year oak.

Soon the shadow catchers arrived, dressed in black. There were two of them, and they wore long black cloaks with pointy black hoods. One couldn't miss them if they tried. They slowly entered the woods, keys jangling from their belts. The keys were for the cage they would place the shadows in once they were caught. This was a special cage with mirrors for walls and a strong light in the center. This cage was a shadow's worst nightmare, for there was nowhere to hide inside.

Pinky and Quizzle's shadows shuddered in the dark. They looked way up into the bright sky, hoping Quizzle and Pinky would wake up. Now that they were scared, they stayed very still, watching as the shadow catchers spread out in their search.

The shadow catchers carried bright lanterns. These lanterns cast light where no light would normally be. The shadow catchers were very organized and carefully searched row by row. All sorts of shadows, large and small, scurried away; but these shadow catchers were interested only in a particular two. They looked carefully, with keen eyes that no one could see, as they swung their lanterns in the air. Tension mounted in the woods as each wakeful soul tried to hide his or her shadow. All the shadows, both large and small, clung tightly to their assigned bodies and tried to blend in.

"You'd better watch out! The Shadow Catchers are coming for you!"

One of the shadow catchers pulled out a scroll and made a formal announcement. "We have a warrant for the shadows of Quizzle the fairy and Pinky Palm the everyanimal, and we demand you step into the light...*now*!"

Quizzle and Pinky's shadows whispered a prayer in the dark. "Wake up you two; we need you!"

The shadow catchers' hoods perked up. They had heard this whispered entreaty in the dark. They began to move towards a long shadow in which the two most likely hid. The tables had turned on this naughty two. Down on dark knees, they prayed for forgiveness for their rude behaviour. It was to no avail. The shadow catchers were approaching closer and closer. They were nearer than near, their lanterns a leer. They seemed to sway in the light and finally spotted the quivering two. Pinky's shadow looked at Quizzle's shadow, and Quizzle's shadow looked at Pinky's shadow. All hope was lost! They were done for.

The shadow catchers opened their cage, and using a bright net, they scooped up the two. Just as they were being placed in the cage though, something shifted in the world of dreams.

As they woke up, Pinky and Quizzle were reunited with their shadows and suddenly found themselves surrounded by mirrors. At first, they each felt a little embarrassed, though they didn't know why. Their shadows clung to them ever so tightly. In the mirror, Quizzle noticed a spike of her hair falling down and brushed it right back into place. Naturally, just having woken from a beautiful dream, Pinky and Quizzle were quite confused.

The shadow catchers saw that these fugitive shadows now each had a body to whom they belonged, and according to the rules, they were forced to release the two. They did so, and then bid them goodbye. Neither Pinky nor Quizzle had a clue about what had gone on. Now, however, it was time to go, and they thanked the trees for the hospitality and the dew.

The trees most graciously said, "Oh, do come again," with bemused smiles. Quizzle and Pinky waved goodbye to the lot and to all of the creatures they'd seen. They flew up to the little robin's nest and bid her a fond adieu, too. Then off they flew. Whew!

As Pinky and Quizzle sailed over the land, their shadows were more than happy to accompany them. Their wings seemed to expand across the whole of Tree Forest as they cruised into the night. Pinky flew Quizzle directly to her door and bid her more sweet dreams. As he climbed into bed at the end of his day, he saw a strange sight. His shadow gave him a nod and a grin and then tucked itself eagerly in. Pinky's shadow had had enough fun for one day.

Hmm, thought Pinky, then off to dreamland he flew. Sweet dreams to all.

This slide was a magical glide... they never knew just where they would end up.

The Slippery Slide

Everyone from Justaroundthebend and the surrounding forest waited for their turn on the Slippery Slide. Each wanted a ride. Now it's important to appreciate that this was no ordinary slide. This slide was a magical glide, for when someone stepped on and then let go, they never knew just where they would end up.

It was Millie Mole's turn, and she stood at the top, looking down the drop. Millie was so nervous that her teeth chattered and her knees felt weak. She feared she might even faint. She held onto the rail with her tiny hands and wouldn't let go. Her knuckles were white with fright.

"It's okay Millie, you can do it!" the onlookers called encouragingly. Millie looked down at Ricky Rabbit and all her friends lined up on the ground. She took a deep breath of fresh air. She uncurled one finger, and another, and her left thumb and then her right thumb, until she was hands-free. She took one nervous little step on the platform towards the slide, and everyone repeated, "You can do it, Millie. We know you can!"

I can do this! thought Millie. "I really can! I can. I can," she said with each tentative step. Then she sat down and prepared to push off.

"I *caaaaaaaaaaaaaaaaaaaan*," was the last word she said before she slipped by.

Where did Millie go, one wonders? In truth, anyone who uses the Slippery Slide has no idea just where they'll end up, a part of the thrill of the ride. Millie went quite quickly. She squealed, jittering all the way down, until she came to an abrupt little stop on the ground. "My goodness! Where am I?" she wondered. She looked around, and what she did see was her very first sight. Millie's mother smiled a big smile.

"Welcome home, Millie!" she said lovingly.

Now, Millie had not seen her mom for quite a while, at least not in this version of reality. Oh, that magical slide! Millie had gone back in time. There were cookies baking in the oven, her favorite kind, and they filled the air with a sweet smell. Millie was little again, perhaps only four weeks old. Her mother picked her up and cuddled her close. With a tear in her eye, Millie's mom sang her a lullaby. Millie felt so warm and safe in her dear mother's arms. She had faced her fear at the top of the ride, and now she felt all good inside. Together, they waited for the cookies to bake.

Now it was TT's turn on the slide. He stood at the top, gazing down towards the ground. He was a little nervous, too, not knowing just where his final destination might be. With some encouragement from all his new friends, TT stepped up and sat himself down. He placed one foot on the slide and then another until there were ten big toes wiggling in front of his green and blue face. TT looked down at Rock, who gave him a nod; and in a blink, he was off. TT didn't squeal or call out, not a "*Boo*!" nor a "*Hoo*!" Down, down, down he went at top speed, his brown hair blowing in the wind and a happy grin on his face. TT entered a world where he had been before. He was very surprised to hear some familiar voices. The voices came from on top of his bridge. It was *the three billy goats Gruff*! He'd been given a second chance, and this time, he wouldn't be fooled; but he just might be kind.

"Who's that *trip-trapping*, *trip-trapping* over my bridge?" he called out, delighted with his fresh start.

"Who's up next?" called out Mayor Justintime.

"I do believe it's my turn," said Mr. Grumpkin, ever so politely, as he stepped up for his ride. Mr. Grumpkin straightened his bowtie and smoothed out his shirt. Wherever he would eventually go, he wanted to present himself in a favorable way. Mr. Grumpkin looked ever so smart in his new suit and his little red hat. Mayor Justintime pinned a red matching rose to the lapel of Mr. Grumpkin's vest. A fine figure of a gnome, some thought, as he sailed on his way. When Mr. Grumpkin's ride came to a stop, he opened his eyes to his best ever surprise.

"Ethel!" he cried. Mrs. Ethel Grumpkin, Fred's long-lost wife, smiled a sweet smile and reached out to accept his offer of a rose. They gazed into each other's glowing faces, remembering all the joys they had shared. Mr. Grumpkin was in heaven, and there he hoped to stay, at least for a while.

"Next?" called out the mayor, as Snake slid over the very last step to the slide's platform.

"I'm here! I'm here!" he called to the mayor as he slid right into place. Snake loved a good ride. "Wee!" he said, thrilled, as he shot down the slippery slide. Snake wiggled and *ziggled* and twisted and turned, laughing and giggling all the way. This was so much more fun for him than it might have been because now he had his S.

Snake landed safely in the dewy morning grass in the Garden of Everywhere. It appeared he'd been given the honor of turning the soil in the fairies' magic garden. In return for this enviable task, he was to be paid a small but powerful wish. As Snake twisted and turned his way through the lovely moist earth, he wondered what he could ever wish for. He was so happy with things just as they were.

Then Ricky Rabbit hopped to the starting point. He tightened his belt up a notch and wiggled his whiskers as he stepped boldly right to the edge. Ricky looked down at the long, silvery slide. Ricky's big feet looked just like skis, and he had decided to go down the run standing up, just for kicks. After a moment, Ricky was ready and pushed himself off.

The whole town cheered. "Way to go, Ricky Rabbit!"

Ricky kept his eyes open the whole slippery way, speeding full-steam ahead into his future. Suddenly, Ricky was standing at the altar with a grown-up Millie Mole. It was their wedding day. Ricky had secretly wondered if she'd say yes when the time came, but it was just too soon, so he scampered away all ablush. Millie smiled a knowing smile and decided she'd go back and wait for a while.

Mayor Justintime pointed at Hummingbird, who waited in line next to Dragonfly. "It's your turn," she said.

Hummingbird hummed up to the entry spot and hung in the air. Dragonfly tried to buzz and nudge in right behind.

"One at a time," called out Mayor Justintime. "Careful dears," she said. "Just one at a time!"

Hummingbird stopped humming and dropped onto the slide. Hummingbird looked so small on this ride, but she was determined to have her slip slide. Then off she went with a whispering *whirr* as her feathers fluffed up in the wind. Dragonfly quickly stepped up, too, and buzzed down. He wanted to catch up with Hummingbird, and so he left in a rush without any fuss. Dragonfly did catch up, and together they shared the best part of the ride. When they came to a stop with a whirr and a buzz, they saw they had more friends that looked just like them. At first, each thought it was themselves they could see. Hummingbird and Dragonfly both buzzed and whirred with pure joy.

"Hey look," they each said. "There's someone like me!"

The line for the slide was still very long, as the folks of Justaroundthebend each awaited their chance. Many of the grown-ups took a turn, too. Mr. Penny had closed the store for this day, missing a great business opportunity in favor of fun. Waiting his turn, hands in his pockets, he jingled his coins. Old Mr. Salamander and Old Lady Muskrat sat watching from two folding chairs. They had already taken their ride on this slide. In the long line, there were some chirpy little chipmunks and some pocket mice, too. Auntie Hoolahoop stood right in the loop. Quizzle and Pinky's parents surveyed the scene, as they liked to know at the end of the day where their children had been. Judge Justapeek was near to the end of the line, and there, in front of the judge waited Skunk and Grupple with their tails in the air.

It was Rock's turn now, and with a gentle push from a friend he rolled right to the edge. Rock, the old soul, was really more interested in the ride than in where he'd arrive. Rock enjoyed just being on this slippery slide. With eyes wide open and a wise knowing grin, Rock gave a wink and was off in a blink!

There was one individual in the line whom one might not have expected, though. Wag! She had heard tell of this *slide along fun*! Her invisible dress was a mess that no one could see. A cold chill transformed the air as she butted right into the front of the line without waiting for her turn. Slipped under her dress was a rattler tattler or two, along for the ride, as one might say. Wag cackled out loud as the town's folk looked everywhere, trying to place the sound. No one could see her, and so the town's folk shook their heads. Wag's toes curled onto the slide along ride, her fly-by-night broom at her side. She was prepared for her descent, and down, down, down she went. Needless to say, she was in for a rough little ride. There was no telling where Wag would come out.

Mayor Justintime called out, "Mrs. Grupple's turn," and the pooch scrambled right up but waited until someone threw her a bone. She chased that bone down the slide, and her flea friends came along, along for the ride.

When she at long last came to a skidding stop, she was greeted by a whole forest of trees that said, "Please do come right in."

Mrs. Grupple was welcome, and she knew this for sure as she nosed her way through. There, in the woods, was another dog. Mrs. Grupple sniffed this new pooch, and, according to protocol, the pooch sniffed right back. Mrs. Grupple offered a warm *shake-a-paw* as her new friend waggled *their* waggly tail.

Mayor Justintime even had the pleasure of sending Judge Justapeek and the entire Gingerbread Council off. Then came her adorable flock of fledglings, each of whom had politely waited their turns. Now it was Auntie Hoolahoop's turn for a ride on the sloping slide. With a wand and a whisper, she bounced herself down to the lip of the slide, and then off she went, her wings tucked in tight. Auntie Hoolahoop was holding a kindly eagle's feather, which she meant to return if she landed just right.

By and by, the whole town's population had taken their turn, until there were only two left. The sun was just beginning to set in Tree Forest when Pinky and Quizzle flew up to the top of the slide. Mayor Justintime had gone just in time. Now Quizzle and Pinky could go as a team.

Quizzle's translucent wings gave a flutter, and Pinky looked down the chute, coming out with a whistle that seemed to say, "Oh my! What a very long way!"

Quizzle looked at Pinky, and Pinky looked at Quizzle with a smile. They joined hand and paw, and they set off into a glide! Quizzle and Pinky sailed up into the night sky! They became shooting stars in a world sweet with dreams.

The slippery slide had offered a ride to everyone who waited. All of the townsfolk slid home—to the home in their hearts. Would you like a ride on this slippery slide?

About the Author

Teresa Mae Waterland, M. Ed., Clinical Counsellor, is on a journey of awareness that includes a passion for fairies—many of whom live just down the lane from her home in the woods. Teresa has extensive training and experience in Drama, English, Psychology, and Broadcasting. Her awareness training in Voice Dialogue, Psychodrama, and Somatic Experiencing have helped her to bring unique perspectives to her work. Teresa declares: if there is only one reality—as many of our great teachers have said—then this must, of course, include fairies and their magical friends.

CPSIA information can be obtained
at www.ICGtesting.com
Printed in the USA
JSHW041503300623
43607JS00001B/7